The CYCLE of CYRNOS

INK START MEDIA
5710 W Gate City Blvd Ste K #284
Greensboro, NC 27407

Isula Rossa
(Île Rousse)
Calvi
Monte Cinto
Corte
Aiacciu
(Ajaccio)
Propriano
Porto-Vecchio
Bonifaziu
(Bonifacio)

The CYCLE of CYRNOS

Book Two The Foundation

By Pascal Paul Piazza

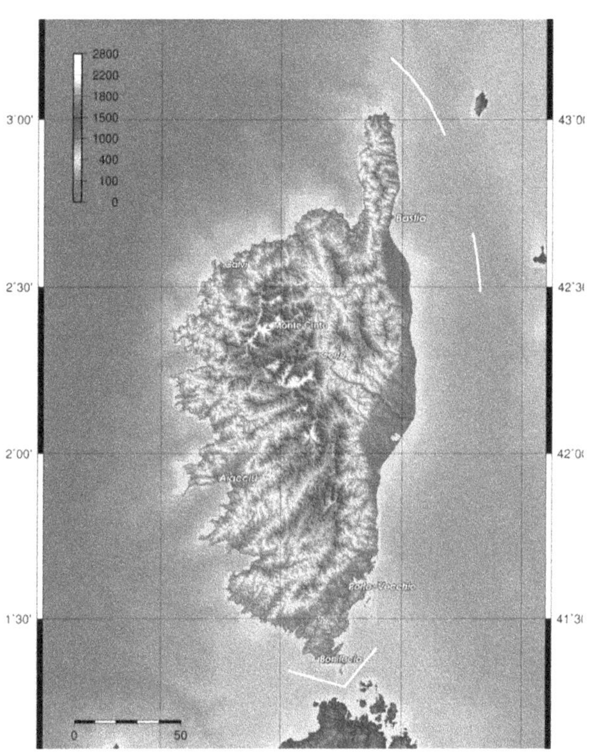

2800
2200
1800
1500
1000
400
100
0
3°00'
2°30'
2°00'
1°30'
43°00
42°30
42°00
41°30
Bastia
Calvi
Corte
Ajaccio
Porto-Vecchio
Bonifacio
0
50

INTRODUCTION

In a corner of the world,
There is a sparkle of tenderness.
Inside my heart, majestic.
It fills you with purity.
Jewel of wonders.
Don't look for similar.
You won't find another alike.
It's unique, alone and dear.

Petru Guelfucci Corsica

Look at your brother.
A chain tightens him.
The same that you bear.
And that oppresses all of us.
If we stretch it all together.
Perhaps someday it will break
And we will make a roar, a roar, a roar.
That will resound around the sea.
If we stretch all together.
Perhaps someday it will break.
And we will make a roar, a roar, a roar.
Like a song of freedom.
Talk to your brother.
We need to prepare the future.
The strength that holds us.
Is only a common idea.

Chjami Aghialesi and Jenifer La Catena

Sing in our language
Sing to say that you are Corsican.
Sing about hope.
Sing about our differences.
Sing in Corsican, sing.

Sing also with the voice of your heart.
Sing about friendship and honor.
Sing about the diaspora.
Who are abandoned by love.
Sing about the Corsican land.

Sing for the future of the Corsicans.
Sing against the poverty.
Sing as a prayer.
Sing, Sing, Sing.
Sing in Corsican Sing.

Michael Mallory Canta

The Corsicans are just to each and live in a more civilized manner than other barbarians… Also in the regulation of the rest of their life, each one in his place observes the laws of rectitude with wonderful faithfulness… The Corsican sense of justice is entirely true and is confirmed by the experience of every age …

Diodorus

Their first law is to revenge themselves.
Their second to live by plunder.
Their third to lie.
Their fourth to deny the gods.

Seneca

Corsicans, even at an early period, were able by their own unaided energies to construct for themselves a democratic commonwealth. The seeds thus planted could never afterwards be eradicated but continued to develop themselves under all of the storms that assailed them, ennobling the rude vigor of a spirited and warlike people, encouraging them through every period an unexampled patriotism and a heroic love of freedom.

Ferdinand Gregorovius
Wandering through Corsica:
Its History and its Heroes: Volume I

The natural formation of the country – ranges of high mountains, with but few passes, intersected by long valleys in which the villages are situated – rendered the pieves practically so many small states. … Freedom … became their ideal, and for some time their influence was on the side of the patriots.

L.H. Caird The History of Corsica

It must be admitted that they have always been revengeful, but they are, as a race, religious, hospitable and honest.

L.H. Caird The History of Corsica

I wish to sleep on Corsican soil.
One last time for eternity.

Michael Mallory Terra Corsa

TABLE OF CONTENTS

CHAPTER TEN

Procession at Filitosa

Filitosa

Corsica: Early Bronze Age 1500 BCE

HYPERBOLEUM

"Oh, granite-schist stone set in a teal sea.

Tied to the mainland yet apart and free.

Crucible to cultures, forests and tales.

Lure to all the ships in calm seas or gales."

DELERIUM

"Twelve tribes occupy inland and the coast.

Hunting, herding, farming and fishing most.

Subsistence builds equal character traits.

Villages track terraces, vines and gates."

PESSIMISSIUM

"Trade is robust welcoming many sails.

There are wood, honey, resin and wax sales.

Pots are made with cut chords and soft sea shells.

Truth from west and east links the two-way trails."

MARY

"North and south villages trade with nearby land.

Purple sails explore west in ships so grand.

The Sherden come east in need of a dock.

All shipping lanes lead to and from this rock."

CHARLOTTE

"Cities like in Ur are not to be found.

But dolmens and menhirs transform the ground.

Standing stones like Carnac dot the southwest.

This tradition was longer than the rest."

CELTS/GAULS

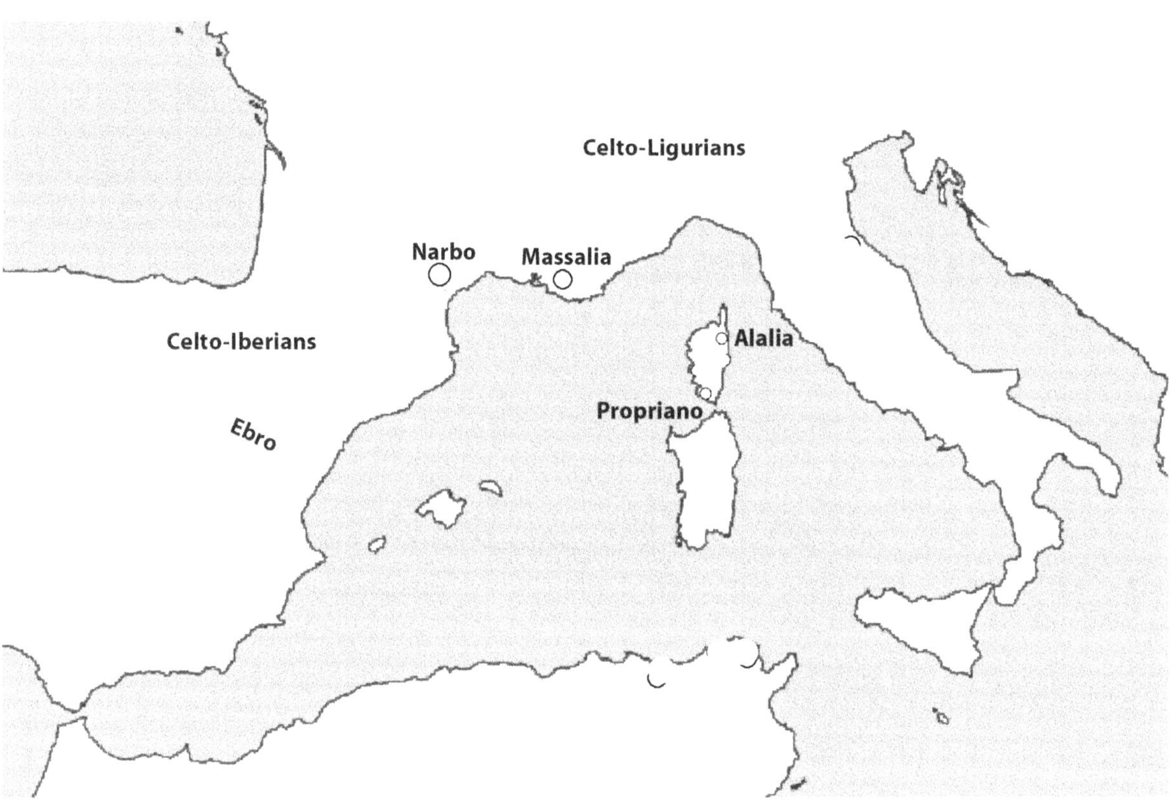

WESTERN MEDITERRANEAN -1500 BCE

Pratu and His Daughter, Luna, Join In the Torch Procession from Propriano to the Standing Stones at Filitosa

PRATU

"When are trees ablaze, but not on fire?

Walk closely as we go ever higher.

Follow the sulphur smoke on our ancient trail.

"Til we reach the path to the stones' tale."

LUNA

"When our torch flames burn brightly on the path.

I know the answer to avoid any wrath.

But, you ask me as if I were a child.

I care for what I see not stories wild."

PRATU

"You are sixteen and know more than I know.

Yet, you do not see the faith the stones sow.

From Carnac to here we express our life.

Dolmens and menhirs cover joy and strife."

LUNA

"I see the Sun align in true measure.

Cold directional stones shape a treasure.

I do not see spirits or Deb's spiteful hand.

These are not men stone frozen in the land."

PRATU

"Life explodes from villages to the coast.

We share a bond and succulent roast.

We are twelve tribes but seek a common bond.

The stones link us from forests to still pond."

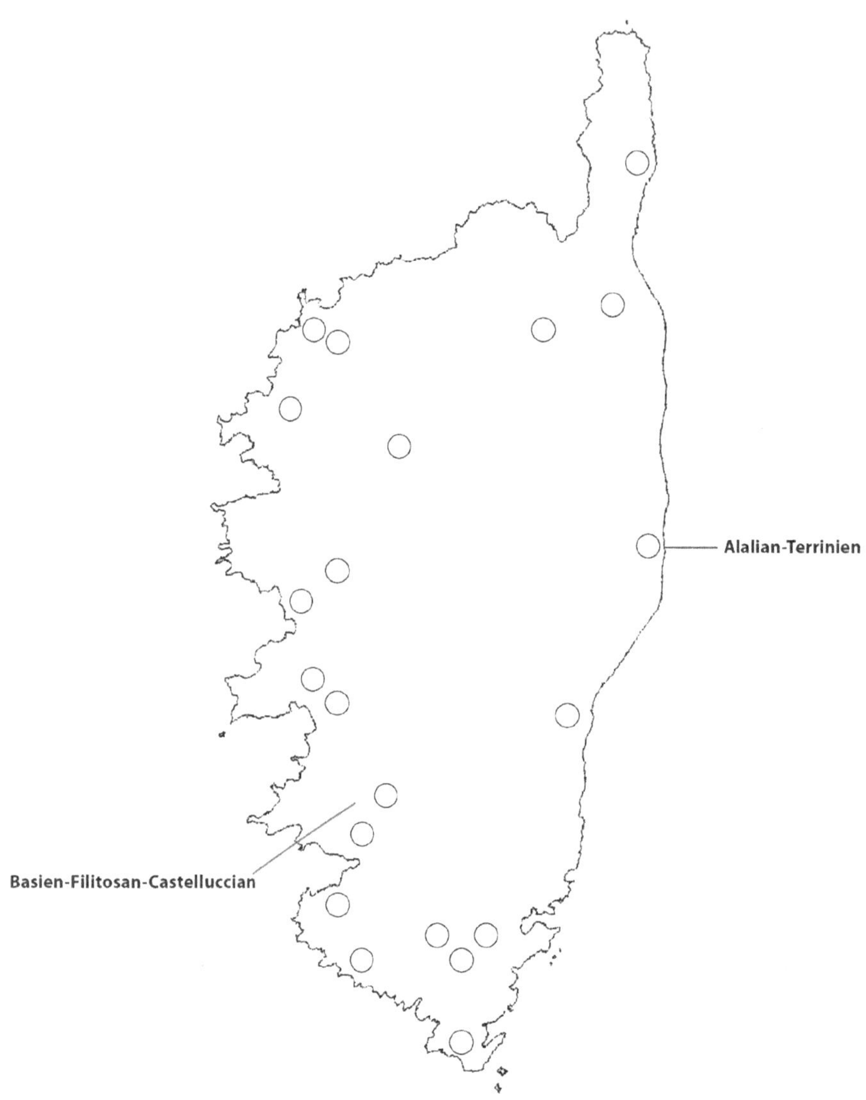

*LATE NEOLITIC-CHALCOLITHIC-EARLY BRONZE AGE
SETTLEMENT PATTERNS*

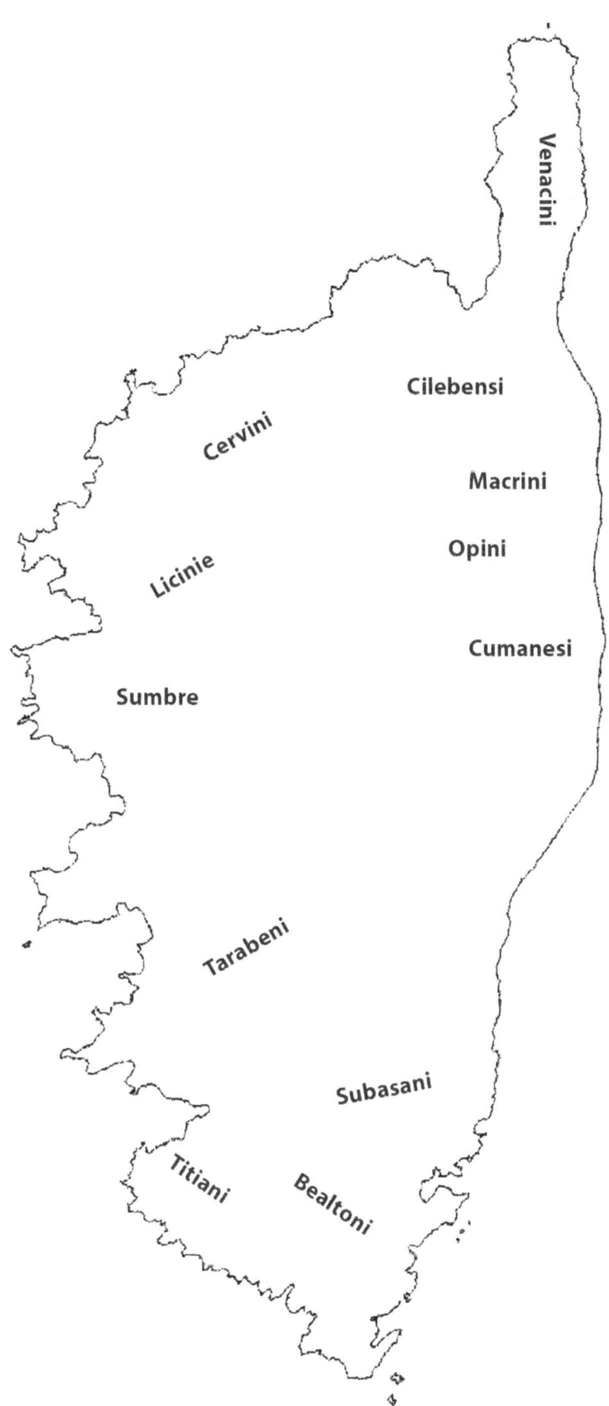

THE TWELVE ANCIENT TRIBES OF CORSICA

Pratu and Luna Met Deb in the Procession

D E B

"Who questions now if I exist this day?
Are these stones just some hurdles in our way?
You are wise beyond youth with much to learn.
There is more to life than how it may turn."

L U N A

"I always knew that you really did exist.
Yet, doubts of you changing shapes still persist.
Your fluid form mirrors stones short and long.
Forming a foundational base so strong."

P R A T U

"She is her mother from whom truth did flow.
Who knew to hunt, herd, gather and then grow.
Asking how crops repeat and the Sun rise?
When will rains come without any surprise?"

D E B

"I knew her well before she left and died.
The stones and the earth had no choice but cry.
I am here because clouds may soon turn black.
Two foes with many ships soon will be back."

L U N A

"The U-shaped port welcomes ships to dock.
Wind and waves succumb to the granite rock.
Open to all that seek trade in our goods.
Or prime for men to fight on docks or in woods."

**Deb Leads Pratu and Luna to the Port of Propriano Where
They Meet Hanno the Elder (a Phoenician Leader) and Sisera (a Sherden Leader)
Competing Warriors and Traders**

PRATU

"The Sun arose to forty ships in the bay.

Split south and north out of the other's way.

Half purple sails from the east fit to fight.

Half white sails from the west of equal might."

DEB *(Transforming Into A Boar Next To Luna)*

"Troops deploy along the opposite bank.

The weight of armor pulses each port plank.

Why have they chosen this day to make war?

I will transform into a vicious boar."

LUNA

"Troops, do not fight this girl and her large pet.

There is time for peace as you have not met.

We do not fear bows or bronze swords or spears.

But, cruel hubris blinds minds and closes ears."

HANNO THE ELDER

"We are not here to fight anyone this day.

We lost most of our food along the way.

We want circle-chord pots with salted meat.

And skins of water to slake certain heat."

SISERA

"We too are not here to start a new fight.

We always lust for the beauty in sight.

We stop because we love the port and place.

We rest before the race quickens the pace."

HANNO THE ELDER

"Our ships have come here with our goods to trade.

They and we are not pirates on a raid.

We sail south of where the Ebro does flow.

Not where Sherden, Celt or Greek grow."

SISERA

"We will pass many purple sails back east.

Today, we will join them in a festive feast.

We go straight east to Egypt for its gold

Not to change trade lanes for goods to be sold."

PRATU

"We sought to act based on what we could see.

Two armed navies docked from the Sea.

Truth often lies beyond the eye's own sight.

Let us enjoy food and friends 'thru the night."

DEB

"We shall erect some stones to mark this day.

They will tell a tale with so much to say.

Today's strong peace must soon not be lost.

To do so will come with an awful cost."

LUNA

"I remain young with one more thing to know.

The stones do speak a certain truth to show.

Faith is logic when facts are certain.

Truth may hide behind an opaque curtain."

Pratu Escorts Byblos the Elder (a Phoenician Leader)
From the Stunning Standing Stones of Filitosa to the Extraordinary Array of
Dolmens and Menhirs South of Propriano

BYBLOS THE ELDER

"The world is a large stretched oval sea.

We sail with the Sun to this island free.

We call it Korsai because of its woods.

We trade for its cardial pots with goods."

PRATU

"Cor and Sica gave us our first name.

Our vast trees also gave us some fame.

We refer to us as Kors meaning wood.

Sica still is our mother as she would."

BYBLOS THE ELDER

"We come from where trees might as well be gods.

Wooden ships built us up against all odds.

Our trade extends beyond the world's boundary.

Embracing every natural foundry."

PRATU

"The trees surround the port like a seine net.

Filtering land paths and keeping them set.

There are many guarded ports just like here.

Nature protects herself both far and near."

BYBLOS THE ELDER

"I want to see a mountain village scene.

How do the tribes live a life so serene?

We too have tribes, but they can only fight.

Peace needs an empire and its full might."

PRATU

"The plains of aligned stones is our first stop.

Down a series of paths that rise and drop.

Six sets of edge stones will direct our way.

Side by side rows mark the time of each day."

BYBLOS THE ELDER

"The large stone tradition is on decline.

The rest of the world has moved down the line.

Building towers and temples and the rest.

Pyramids and ziggurats are now best."

PRATU

"It remains here, as it is who we are.

See, the great pi dolmen with its cross bar.

Each tribe supports the rest staying higher.

We only stand due to the forge of fire."

BYBLOS THE ELDER

"Great houses express strength and pure power.

That dominion must have a high tower.

Each stone here is equal in width and height.

There is no feeling who is best and right."

PRATU

"Subsistence is like a stone hard and cold.

Strong and straight and unable now to fold.

See Pelaggiu's stones beckon us now to try.

Our stones are like stars in the black night sky."

MEGALITHIC ALIGNMENTS, DOLMENS, MENHIRS AND COFFERCIST TOMBS PRINCI- PALLY AROUND FILITOSA AND THE CAURIA PLATEAU

Palaggiu Alignments

Palaggiu Alignment

Santori Alignment

Renaghju Alignment

*There are Torre (Towers) Which are Part of
the Tradition of the Sardinian Nuraghi (Towers) and Obsidian Trade,
Which Overlook the Menhirs, and Which are Controlled by Chiefs and Not Villages*

BYBLOS THE ELDER

"But down there I see a tower or two.

Commanding the whole plain and now our view.

Twins to nuraghi on Sardinia's coast.

A seamless tradition for you to boast?"

PRATU

"The black glass we buy comes with ideas too.

So, towers appear, but only a few.

In each hamlet next to each new tower.

A brash chief rule alone with full power."

BYBLOS THE ELDER

"That is the way of the civilized state.

Rulers rule firm and the rest lay prostrate.

It is the way and order of all things.

Protection comes with the kissing of rings."

PRATU

"This island will not allow that to occur.

The sheep run free in full sight of the cur.

Armies may conquest the coast with some ease.

The maquis cannot be tamed only tease."

BYBLOS THE ELDER

"Someday, the tower will show its great worth.

It will symbolize the land of your birth.

Enjoy your freedom as long as you can.

The Sun still sets before the race is ran."

Pascal Paul Piazza

On the East Coast of Corsica, Intrepidu Meets with Atromitos (a Greek Trader) Selling the Pottery and Goods of a Local Corsican Tribe (the Terriniens) Amid a Visit by Deb

ATROMITOS

"Your honey, wax and resin are the best.

Your pots are better than all of the rest.

Incised chorded blackware sell on their own.

They make the best first trade seeds to be sown."

INTREPIDU

"Our products are sourced from mountain towns.

Seasoned on the roads here both up and down.

The coastal plain supplies us the clay for pots.

Artists groove upside down chevrons and dots."

ATROMITOS

"How do you secure your source of supply?

When all hives and plants commonly lie?

Does no one steal what your sources may find?

When your wares are simply one of a kind?"

INTREPIDU

"The person who finds a hive owns it alone.

Cow bears brands even in a common zone.

No one would steal the comb or the bees.

They husband each other's cows and fruit trees."

ATROMITOS

"That is a fair and forthright way to act.

Your reputation is a truthful fact.

Our trade flourishes and grows on demand.

Thanks to the communal supply on hand."

INTREPIDU

"How do you market the products bought here?

What brand applies to products without peer?

You sell to all heirs of Sica and Cor.

But what true name begs them to ask for more?"

ATROMITOS

"We use Kalliste or beautiful isle.

It is like a woman of winsome wile.

Or, Cyrnos where fabled Kurnos did stay.

Chasing sea nymphs and drinking wine all day."

INTREPIDU

"Has our legacy been lost over time?

That nations invent a new tale or rime?

Cor and Sica were an intrepid pair.

Having their name preserved is only fair!"

ATROMITOS

"Troy now is the city the world most loves.

So, Prince Corsus first arrived with doves.

He was also known as Hercules' son.

Truth is not as important as deeds done."

INTREPIDU

"The twelve tribes here have lost memory too.

Corsica comes from the Corsu tribe true.

Or, from Kors which means wood in our text.

Who knows what new names will be used next?"

ATROMITOS

"What will not change is the pure solid rock!

That forms this island from mountain to dock.

The tribes are the same wherever I have been.

Keeping separate but always one kin."

INTREDIPU

"Trees look like trees, but a fir is not a pine.

Granite seems like schist without mica's shine.

Two-thirds is magma from Pangea's rift.

The rest came with the Alps and a plate shift."

DEB

"I was there to watch the new island rise.

It was quite an amazing fire surprise

I will never forget the day of its birth.

When magma shot forth from under the earth"

DEB

"I was swimming when Corsica was made.

Zeus long observed me hiding in the shade.

Hera was fuming of Zeus's lust for me.

She had Hades raise fire through the Great Sea."

DEB

"Molten rock spew forth with a sulphur plume.

Molding granite ribs of a new Typhon.

Zeus threw a bolt freezing the ribs in place.

Making an island in an empty space."

D E B

"Zeus then pushed the plate with all his might.

Impacting the mainland made such a sight.

Mountains arose where before there were none.

This was the sharp start of what would be done."

D E B

"Part of the sea floor went under the land.

Part folded back in a manner so grand.

Zeus laid the fold over a granite gap.

Forming the east plains and the single cap."

D E B

"Zeus then formed the sleek shape of the isle.

I will infuse such beauty in each mile.

All will know the Venus that I did prize.

I spent my power making this isle rise."

D E B

"Hera smiled, as I finished my swim.

She had frustrated Zeus' caprice and whim.

Not in the manner that she had sought.

But, Zeus knew too well that he had been caught."

D E B

"Hera still had no good reason to fear.

I would not be some willing swan or deer.

Yet, I found a new home to be alone.

And a new place to reflect and atone."

ATROMITOS

"So, the cap and east connect by the Sea.

The mainland is their own twin family.

This third has its own different birthright.

Its own sphere of influence day and night."

INTREPIDU

"The cap is still different than the east.

Hidden villages with their wild boar feast.

Terraced fields form a patchwork of fresh foods.

Interspersed among the path and woods."

ATROMITOS

"I know the east and its expansive plain.

It is a trade hub that should never wane.

The rest may withdraw from the outside pace.

Someday, Greeks will make a home of this place."

INTREPIDU

"The Corsu would all welcome its old friend.

Our two traditions would easily blend.

The trade route would expand and it would grow.

Where it goes to is what we want to know?"

ATROMITOS

"North to Etruria trading wax for belts.

West to Massalia to buy from the Celts.

Next to Narbo and the Ebro for sure.

Then, return to our home with bronze so pure."

CUNLIFFE

"The Bronze Age was a turning point in trade.

Repeat sales soon replaced the random raid.

Commerce networks composed the land and Sea.

Crucibles of exchange but not for free."

KRISTIANSEN

"Metal was the catalyst for such change.

Bronze forms from alloys at a high heat range.

Made from copper and tin found far apart.

That is how the growing trade spheres did start."

RENFREW

"Copper from the Ebro was highly sought.

Fused to tin from Britain recently bought.

A Celtic forge blends a bronze sword so bold.

Sold to a chief in the vast Jutland cold."

SUCHOWSKA

"Amber arises north of the wide Rhine.

It buys island ingots and jars of wine.

It wanders alone through the Lions Gate.

Having pivoted to set the Danube's fate."

DE MORTILLET

"The path of amber fuels the fate of tribes.

A story that was written by the scribes.

Goths, Visi and Vandals head south to roam.

One thousand years hence they will become Rome."

Renaghju Alignment

CHAPTER ELEVEN

The Roman Quintet: The Siege of Filitosa 1200 BCE

HYPERBOLEUM

"The Great Sea pulses to play its own part.

It cradles us who have sailed from the start.

It covers the wrecks of hubris and bile.

It cures with salt, brine and a whimsy wile."

DELERIUM

"Waves sing to entice us to give up care.

We are blind to the tempest lurking there.

Yet, there is no peace like rest on a beach.

Or, chasing the sun-arc within our reach."

PESSIMISSIUM

"Magic lives to conjure our own sea path.

Ships sail to open love, envy and wrath.

The sea taunts us when we need a drink

It washes sweat when we need time to think."

MARY

"We may be frogs by a pond for our sea.

Clay words chart what we want and know to be.

Did we travel west and go east one day?

Or just the opposite, can we now say?"

CHARLOTTE

"Gaps still cloud the answer to what we ask.

Cyrnos has to be where we start our task.

It saw battles of heroes and wood ships.

It set the tone of all of our dreams and trips."

Deb Tries to Relax in the Sea Off Brandu But Has Premonitions of an Imminent Battle In Propriano

D E B

"The Great Sea slowly scars with a boast.

It cut many coves forming a coarse coast.

Each was a refuge restful and restive.

Wood walls of trees are secure and festive."

D E B

"The cove at Brandu is where I must think.

I cup the clear cure of cold water to drink.

I loosen my tunic and lay to rest.

I find the peace of the rock at its best."

D E B

"I have taken many shapes in my life.

I was an ibex that cured Cor's strife.

I was a cave mystic that gave him hope.

I was a girl with a flower to cope."

D E B

"I may just rest and stare for a whole day.

I cannot resist the lure of the spray.

I cannot because the sea is my soul.

If I do not swim it will takes its toll."

D E B

"The foam forms under me when I now rise.

I start to swim and find a new surprise.

A sublime shape matches my stroke for stroke?

A dolphin laughs and plays as if I joke."

D E B

"My fulsome fear forms first fast and then slow.

Amplitude of thoughts pulse high and low.

Sensing what may arise comes with a price.

Fear feeds my thoughts and the sea is my spice."

D E B

"There has been balance across the Great Sea.

Babu's rule had been the trigger and key.

Cities, art and trade left the high hills.

They rose among the rivers with such skills."

D E B

"Menhirs and dolmens bonded tribes out west.

The lure of the east was still a great test.

The Sherden found Cyrnos on their way east.

Sea People who saw each shore as a feast."

D E B

"Punic tribes in the east were rich from shells.

Purple goods went west on ships with full sails.

Protis sought the arc-end of the Sun's path.

His ships sought to bypass the Punic wrath."

D E B

"But, there is something wrong that makes me fear.

The balance was fragile during each year.

Like the Sea still water can become rough.

Charting a path among high waves is tough."

Zittu and Novu are the Corsican Sentinels for the Port for Filitosa

ZITTU

"Boredom is as thick as our granite stand.

Fog lifts to the same boats about to land.

Cor found his Sica and Babu went east.

We sit. We see. We talk. We mean the least."

NOVU

"You want to come, see and conquer as one.

You miss your own worth without some acts done.

Twelve tribes put us here for many reasons.

Then seek the high maquis for each season."

ZITTU

"I am a hedgehog lost to all I know.

I tread in a cold cage with stone to tow.

I run in place but do not move or do.

Changes are few as the port days renew."

NOVU

"But a hedgehog sees what he has to see.

His focus makes him what he has to be.

I am a fox seeing what else is there.

Do you not see that now or even care?"

ZITTU

"If only you were now a talking fox.

I then would start to think outside the box.

The fog curtain lifts showing an open port.

We have to count again from our own fort."

ZITTU

"The port awakes so be ready to run.

Take this urgent message straight from the Sun.

A boat docks with some fresh fish from the night.

Un-caught fish laugh in the water out of sight."

NOVU

"Why do you mock what peaceful waters mean?

Do you need to see a blood-oil glean?

We are ready when the time is at hand.

We will spread the word for the tribes and land."

ZITTU

"You seek portents and signs among the waves.

You find comfort among these cold stone staves.

A calm cove hides the lesson lost on me.

Waves break over fish for a routine sea."

NOVU

"You can see, but you do not want to think.

I feel the waves will soon crash on a brink.

Connect the points as Cor did on his path.

Calm hides a fierce fury and salty wrath."

ZITTU

"The port will be a blank slate like this rock.

Boats will offload tempting birds on the dock.

Time will track the static tie of a knot.

If I am here with you or if I am not."

Sidon and Tyre, the Phoenician Leaders, Prepare Offshore to Occupy the Port for Filitosa, Although the Elder Tyre and the Younger Sidon Debate the Purpose of the Operation

SIDON

"My brother, the moon mocks the next sun rise.

Lunar light conceals the next great surprise.

The sun will reveal our ships in the port.

The world has not seen anything of this sort."

TYRE

"Waves are calm as we prepare from my ship.

Unlike the storm that demanded this trip.

We must oust the Sherden by true surprise.

Silence the port watch before the sun does rise."

SIDON

"Ba'al gave us this chance to make it right.

We have the men and ships to win a fight.

Hanno squandered his best chance when it came.

Diplomacy fails and hinders one's fame."

TYRE

"My old hip feels the full fear that you lack.

We are not here to pillage and to sack.

Babu's kin are our kin just gone astray.

We come to stop the Sherden on their way."

SIDON

"This island is perfect for a new base.

We would control all commerce at our pace.

We must strike strongly with bronze and fire.

Let Sherden ships and wood forts fuel the pyre."

Sidon and Tyre Meet with the Captains of the Thirty Phoenician Ships

TYRE

"Welcome aboard as we prepare to land.

Like Sidon, you burn hot to mark your brand.

Ba'al keeps the owl not the hawk in sight.

We must think even if we still must fight."

SIDON

"My blood does boil, but we cannot be rash,

The wave now calm seeks the coarse rock to crash.

Go back to your ships and speak these few words.

Lift their spirit to soar high with the birds."

TYRE, SIDON AND ALL CAPTAINS

"We wear the purple to show we are the best.

You sweat, strain and stroke surpassing the test.

From your mother's breast to a wife's last kiss.

You know this is not a chance you can miss."

TYRE, SIDON AND ALL CAPTAINS

"Who we are is at stake and could be lost.

You accept sharp pain and strife at all cost

We are now here to stop the Sheridan's path

Without Babu's heirs incurring our wrath."

TYRE, SIDON AND ALL CAPTAINS

"We will fight though anybody who wants to fight.

Twenty ships and men will secure the land tight.

Ten ships will protect the port from attack.

Frontal rams will force all other ships back."

The Sentinels Zittu and Novu Witness the Arrival of the Phoenicians

Z I T T U

"The Sun's light peaks from under the dark veil.

Little by little there is sand and shell.

What! By Babu! Ships with a stripped sail.

There is wood to see and no fish to smell."

N O V U

"What joke do you conjure to wake me up?

Can I at least have a drink from my cup?

Let me – Oh my! Your wish to act is here.

There is no time to wait or shed a tear."

Z I T T U

"I fear first that I cannot get it done.

I fear next that I do not know how to run.

Maybe the tribes knew better than me.

And left me not to act but just to see."

N O V U

"You can and will act as they knew you would.

You will pass as only the mouflon could.

You are the hedgehog knowing how to go.

You will find where only the wind can blow."

Z I T T U

"You are stronger than our granite rock stand.

You are my soul, as soil is the land.

Yet, you must warn the Sherden without haste.

I must find other tribes to stop this waste."

Pascal Paul Piazza

**The Phoenicians Land in the Port and Track Zittu and Novu
As Zittu and Novu Run to Alert the Twelve Tribes of Corsica**

SIDON

"Store the sails. Set the standard. We are here.

Seal the port. Put the chain from pier to pier.

For the Sherden, this is a wooden weir.

Tell the Corsu that there is nothing to fear."

BYBLOS

"What if they will not heed our words of peace?

What if they think that we are here to fleece?

We have shown a great display of our might.

Would not we regroup and prepare to fight?"

SIDON

"Captain, you just have to make it known.

It is not their land that we seek to own.

Deploy the cohort and get the job done.

They will soon see that we can act as one."

BYBLOS

"The orders are clear and are already in place.

Our troops will soon cover the entire space.

We will use surprise to flange up our ranks.

They will have no choice but to give us thanks."

SIDON

"I hope that same wit extends to your task.

We laugh later when we drink from the cask.

Please stop those runners in your line of sight.

Or, kill them quickly if they flee or fight."

ZITTU

"I hear them yell, but they are out of range.

That they yell first does seem to be quite strange.

The goat path that only I know is near.

That we will soon be en route is quite clear."

NOVU

"Do not let their words detract from your goal.

I will follow as a mare does a foal.

The morning mist and herbs refresh my heart.

I would thus know where I am from the start."

ZITTU

"The path soon arrives, but it is narrow.

We know to expect a sling or arrow.

Outrageous fortune! I felt the first few.

Duck and crawl on belly cold stone and dew."

NOVU

"You go first and I will follow you along.

But wait, I have slipped on stones less strong.

I must stop to rest, but you must go on.

Here is where we part on this dewy dawn."

ZITTU

"I will not leave you, but I know I must.

I feel like I have betrayed your trust.

My duty compels me to leave you now.

I will find you but I do not know how."

**Byblos, a Phoenician General, Finds Novu. Novu Buys Time for Zittu
to Complete His Mission. Novu Kills Her Phoenician Guard.**

BYBLOS

"Woman, why do you lie on the cold ground?

You did not fall. You did not make a sound.

Your ankle is not broken, black, or blue.

Your breast, face and leg glisten in the dew."

NOVU

"Why did you now send the others away?

Do you think your prowess will give you sway?

Get closer and go from small bull to cow.

With my small knife, I will show you how."

BYBLOS

"Are all women here so hostile and mean?

Yet, you fell in a manner to be seen.

Did you so stop so you could insult me?

Or, to buy some time for him to run free?"

NOVU

"Do you think that I would tell you one thing?

You invade and expect the bells to ring.

You will never know the very high ground.

You too will fall on the ground with no sound."

BYBLOS

"No Siren call led us here for some charm.

But, we do not mean to bring any harm.

We are traders against the Sherden way.

We want all of your trade and we will pay."

NOVU

"Do you know why I do not believe you?
Spears and slings do not make a merchant crew.
We cannot hear words when ships seize our port.
We will all fight here and fight from our fort."

BYBLOS

"We hoped our ships would make the right sight.
That you would seek peace rather than to fight.
The last stand will be where the small stones stand.
I leave to start the siege upon the land."

NOVU

"You can leave me, but we will meet once more.
The stones stand sacred both in act and lore.
The Sherden and the tribes will soon be here.
You will be trapped with much more to fear."

PHOENICIAN SOLDIER

"You are not going anywhere at this time.
My siege of you will be written in rime.
You will not die soon, but you wish you had.
You will lose your sense and become so mad."

NOVU

"Then, come close quickly and fall in my arms.
I will reveal the secret of my charms.
May my wound be mortal for all to know?
Your neck bleeds so that freedom will soon grow."

Lowland Maquis

Zittu Falters on the Path, But Meets a Talking Goat

ZITTU

"Where I am on the path is hard to know.

Twists, turns, tumbles test temper high then low.

I am on goat time as I barely walk.

I wish Novu were here so we could talk."

ZITTU

"I am glad that I often pass this way at night.

I feel the edge as if I had no sight.

I grasp and grimace the granite and stone.

The pain prepares me for my way alone."

ZITTU

"How many times have I fallen on the ground?

Blood gathers hiding sharp scrapes all around.

How can I go on when I cannot see?

I sweat in the cold on my neck and knee."

ZITTU

"The arrow digs into my side to bleed.

Good sleep and food is what I now need.

I did not tell Novu that I was struck.

How is it I feel like a hunted buck?"

ZITTU

"A goat would not stop or feel any pain.

A sure hoof would command both ice and rain.

I am not a goat, an ibex or a deer.

I will just rest here and absorb my fear."

A TALKING GOAT

"Zittu, why is it that you soundly sleep?

When there are so many rewards to reap?

Eleven tribes wait for you to arrive.

Twelve tribes rely upon you to survive."

ZITTU

"Why stop my sleep so I should hurt some more?

The point is still sharp piercing and sore.

There is no reason now to look around.

I am alone and can hear no sound."

A TALKING GOAT

"You are as bad as Cor when I met him.

That I talk should entice you from the rim.

That I am here tells you the die is cast.

It is your future to save not your past."

ZITTU

"If what you say is what is meant to be.

You are Deb and we are meant to be free.

Why do I need to finish my long path?

I do not want to suffer any more wrath."

TALKING GOAT

"I did not give any new gift to Cor.

I let him see that he could make new lore.

He and you know what has to be done.

With this balm rest until the next new Sun."

Novu Runs to Find the Sherden While Zittu Runs to find the Other Corsican Tribes.
Novu Searches for Her Path and Meets a Talking Goat.

N O V U

"I run quickly like an ibex in flight.

I must find the Sherden before next light.

I glide gently over the granite stone.

I fly myself but I am not alone."

N O V U

"I know Zittu hid the hurt, blood and harm.

I guess he was hit once below his arm.

He did not want me to know of his plight.

I am not there for him to help him fight."

N O V U

"If I were then caught, he could run fast.

I had oft seen him do that in the past.

But, he always knew I would be there.

He and I work best when we are a pair."

N O V U

"I killed a man that did not harm me.

I had to do it for me to be free.

I would do it again if I must do.

Guile is custom that acts as a strong glue."

N O V U

"My eyes drift 'til they stare into my soul.

A rift in the path has made a great hole.

I will just jump reaching for the far side.

My grasp can look not well beyond my pride."

TALKING GOAT

"Did you really want to end up down there?

Did you not think or did you just not care?

I was surprised to see you on this path.

The gap is a hurdle filled with strong wrath."

NOVU

"Maybe, you could help with a lot less talk.

When I grab the edge I begin to balk.

The stone scratches making my belief wane.

If I stay here I will become insane."

TALKING GOAT

"So, you want to drag me down in the pit.

And, I cannot be clever with my wit.

My magic could make all this go away.

But, then what would you really have to say."

NOVU

"There are many who depend upon me.

I jumped for them because I could see.

There is a path no hole can ever stop.

The bottom is the start to find the top."

TALKING GOAT

"Then, I have given the help that you need.

Grasp the edge to find you can do the deed.

Pull with power now to confront the edge.

Sense the stone to find a support and ledge."

Zittu Appears Before the Before the Council of the Twelve Corsican Tribes

COUNCIL MEMBER

"You were long put in place so we could see.

We stay high alone above the ground and sea.

Quickly, speak now and tell us if you may.

Our patience wanes as does the Sun each day."

ZITTU

"The Punic purge pulsates like a fast flood.

It will cover our home in our own blood.

Eleven other tribes cannot hide now.

Or else be ready to kneel, scape and bow."

COUNCIL MEMBER

"They cannot find us so we cannot lose.

They will meet us only if we so choose.

You fear simply because Novu gave in.

Now, you are afraid that you may not win."

ZITTU

"She was brave, as she let herself be caught.

I had to run for the fight to be fought.

She made that happen now at her own cost.

We must honor her and not a cause lost."

COUNCIL MEMBER

"You are true and have done your job so well.

She must be freed for the stories to tell.

Return, we will join the fight that you so seek.

We will bring all the strong, the brave and meek."

Pascal Paul Piazza

Novu Signals the Sherden Fleet with a Fire and Then Alerts the Sherden to the Phoenician Operation

SHERDEN CAPTAIN

"Whose fire invites me to stop my boat?

You wear no crown or any silken coat.

I must reach the port as soon as I can.

Should I stop for any woman or man?"

NOVU

"Do you want to know why there is a fire?

Maybe, you prefer to find the waiting pyre?

Would my sex matter if Sica were here?

O do you hide that which you now fear?"

SHERDEN CAPTAIN

"So, now you are the mother of us all?

Should I shake, shimmer and start to fall?

Am I picked by the gods as are you?

Find me a goat to kill and make a stew."

NOVU

"We have no time to talk as death is near.

Punic sails set waiting for the ram to shear.

They hold the port and besiege standing stones.

They hope for the Sun to bleach your bare bones."

SHERDEN CAPTAIN

"I bow to truth and guidance that is wise.

We will not walk into their planned vise.

Return, they will not know when we arrive.

They will soon learn Sica's children survive."

45

The Hill at Filitosa

Pascal Paul Piazza

***The Phoenicians Siege the Hill at Filitosa By Encircling the Hill with a Wood Re-enforced
Trench and Marshaling Their Troops and Special Warriors***

SIDON

"The Corsu found a hill where stones still stand.

A fort is small, but rests strong on firm land.

We circle them with a trench six feet deep.

And twelve feet wide no ibex could soon leap."

BYBLOS

"The men wait with patience, but are not bored.

They erect staves both ways and walls of board.

Water is drained so the floor is dry and firm.

They are perched behind the earthen berm."

SIDON

"Let sorties watch and chop wood for the camp.

Time beckons us to move dirt for the ramp.

They must only see our grandeur and might.

We will deter any will to want to fight."

BYBLOS

"Will champions fight to decide the day?

One on one as the men remain at bay.

No one will defeat our Amazon queen.

It will be the greatest combat yet seen."

SIDON

"No, we seek no harm, slaves or land to boot.

This will end without an arrow to shoot.

Our vise will crush the Sherden in the port.

We then open trade with those in the fort."

FILITOSAN ELDER

"How do we fight to get out of this trap?

They have built a noose of a wooden wrap.

Brave men will impale on staves of oak wood.

Bowing to their more men and our less food."

DEB

"I am here as you seem to need some aid.

Your troops are few but they are not afraid.

It may appear darkest before the dawn.

They must think we are as a wounded fawn."

FILITOSAN ELDER

"Having you on the wall gives the men life.

You have power to find strength out of strife.

You could make all of this end in a day.

Let the champions fast settle this fray."

DEB

"That is not how to end this nascent war.

Killing a queen will not even the score.

Blood should not replace water in the casks.

Let Novu and Zittu complete their tasks."

FILITOSAN ELDER

"We have little water left now to wait.

I am too old to sit and wait for Fate.

I listen to you as Pascal did not.

Each hour presents a new twisted knot."

Pascal Paul Piazza

Tyre and Sidon Asks the Filitosan Elder to Parley

SIDON

"The wind is fresh breathing herbs in the air.

It fills our lungs to speak of what is fair.

I talk terms of faith and not men and spears.

I seek oil and a port above all fears."

FILITOSAN ELDER

"The fox charmed the same words to the crow.

Seeking cheese not help from a bird in tow.

Your point is made by the sword and the lance.

Not by a sharp tongue with chords to entrance."

TYRE

"You and I have seen too many suns set.

We soothe scars of the pain we have met.

My men will swarm like locusts on dry grain

Let us not dance in blood but in Spring rain."

FILITOSAN ELDER

"We have sinew forming a knot of pride.

We cannot lose as Deb is on our side.

Staves face front and back so you dare not move.

Looking mean is the plan you did approve."

SIDON

"Your witch is no match for Ama or Zon.

They have never lost and always have won.

We will cover you with black pitch like rain.

Fire is next unless there is peace to gain."

Novu Arrives with the Sherden and Zittu Arrives with Troops from the Other Eleven Tribes Which Encircle the Phoenicians in Their Trench. A Compromise is Reached.

NOVU

"I break into this meeting on the brink.

This parlay is more even than you think.

Sherden ships surround Punic ships and pride.

Soon much wood will float in on the tide."

ZITTU

"You too will not like my sudden entrance.

Tribes circle your trench in a common stance.

You will have to defend both front and back.

There will be no time for you to attack."

DEB

"Ama, Zon and I will fight when we must.

To preserve honor and to restore trust.

We will not draw blood to split up spoils.

There must be a reason for any toils."

FILITOSAN ELDER

"We do not need a talking bird or goat.

We can decide if we make peace or gloat.

Babu is kin to all and the source of life.

We must drink wine not the taste of strife."

TYRE

"I did not want to hurt any tribe or land.

I sought to make a point and take stand.

I would surprise the Sherden to leave this place.

Now, for no reason we share the same space."

The Aftermath of the Battle

D E B

"There was a pact sharing commerce and trade.
There would not be a third time to invade.
Sherdens sail west from where the Ebro flows.
Sticking close to where the Mistral blows."

D E B

"The Punic horde left with no horns or feast.
Sidon and Tyre went home to the east.
Purple sails went west staying to the south.
Leaving a sad bitter taste in their mouth."

D E B

"The tribes went home so as not to be seen.
Safe in the high maquis and brush so green.
Ships and sails may set as the Sun and Moon.
Ports on the coast do not bother them soon."

D E B

"Watchers became heroes of young and old.
Many children heard their bold exploits told.
Novu and Zittu just had to be wed.
Al and Alia came forth form their bed."

D E B

"Feel the stones stand talking as a blank slate.
I know what they say about our past fate.
Let us place stone men to mark our deeds here.
Where reason and bravery overcame fear."

Filitosa with all the monuments

CHAPTER TWELVE

CELTS/GAULS

Battle of Alalia

Pascal Paul Piazza

**The Roman Quintet: It is an Existential Question
Battle of Alalia 540 BCE**

HYPERBOLEUM

"We make the heroes in the epic tale.

We compose the morals and truths to tell.

A routine raid becomes a nation's quest.

Steps on a path transform into a test."

DELERIUM

"We have to forget first and then recall.

It is as if we never knew at all.

A memory can be lost and not found,

Yet still influence us in acts all around."

PESSIMISSIUM

"Time seems like an illusion of brave acts.

A culture loses fiction, lore and facts.

It misses magic making a group unique.

If finds the role of foil its technique."

MARY

"If we are gone, Sica would still meet Cor.

Babu would leave to find something more.

What we say is what we see though not live.

What we live is real as is what we give."

CHARLOTTE

"You speak as if you know what is to be.

We do not want to test if we are the key.

They will seek to destroy this new course.

They will enlist the aid of an old force."

Deb Returns to Brandu and Carries on a Conversation with the Gabbro (a Rock Found There)

D E B

"How can I be hurt when I did not fight?

How can I be blind when I have full sight?

Why do I shake when the staid schist stays still?

Why am I cold when the Sun warms my will?"

B R A N D U ' S   G A B B R O

"Do you not recall where magic is found?

It is there with blood on the cold ground.

You won the war between evil and good.

Losing part of your soul in stone and wood."

D E B

"I do not care why we all fought that day.

The stones still stand with not much to say.

The new stones show the soldiers who fought.

And tell tales of the freedom that was bought."

B R A N D U ' S   G A B B R O

"I have xenoliths that are part of me.

There is no way for me to be set free.

You though can escape your pain and strife.

But pay to the stones a part of your life."

D E B

"That will stop if I stay in Brandu now.

I can rest and swim and not ask why or how.

I follow the dolphins there in the sea.

There is a path as I want to be free."

Al and Alia, The Children of Luna and Zittu, and Their Friend Plato, a Phocaean Greek, Play on the Sea and Meet Deb

PLATO

"Your sister is Artemis bound in chains.

She needs a hunt now to challenge her brains.

She should not be on this or any ship.

She yearns for a wily foe with a quick quip."

AL

"I did not know you saw her in that way.

But, she most wanted to sail this clear day.

She is a lynx looking for some new prey.

Yet, she seeks no new kill, but just to play."

ALIA

"Look at the dolphins school far from shore!

Playful grace as I have not seen before.

Who swims fast as if she has flippers too?

Is she real or mythic nymph in the blue."

PLATO

"Get back in the boat for you cannot drown.

If you are gone, who will guide the town?

I did not know your sister swam so well.

This is a new tale the huntress can tell."

AL

"I am not amazed by what she can do.

What her limits are I haven't a clue.

I am glad she smiles forgetting the pain.

Let the boat moor 'til her frolic will wane."

ALIA

"How do you swim free, yet you do not drown?

Your chestnut hair hides a smirk not a frown.

What cloth do you wear both opaque and sheer?

That protects you from harm both far and near."

DEB

"You are bold to swim so far on the sea.

But, wear this fleece from your neck to your knee.

It forms to your body so you can float.

A little magic, but you can still gloat."

ALIA

"This is a gift that I cannot repay.

I have no cares for the rest of the day.

My brother and I thank you just the same.

To do so, I need to know your true name."

DEB

"I have no name and all names when I dare.

I am the animal that speaks with care.

I am Deb so you may have heard of me.

I am free, yet in chains, as you may see."

ALIA

"I just see a friend who needs to eat soon.

Al prepares food to eat under the Moon.

Plato tell tales such that you will want more.

It is time now to return to the shore."

Pascal Paul Piazza

Al and Plato Head to Shore and Prepare a Meal When Alia and Deb in the Guise of a Cyclops Have
Some Fun with Al and Plato When They Are Joined by Ibefix the Gaul

A L

"We have time to hunt and to seine some fish.

Stoke the fire and find fresh herbs for each dish.

The women will emerge on foam with the tide.

You and I will entertain with such pride."

C Y C L O P S

"Who dare eats my fish and butchers my sheep.

I will bury your blood and bones so deep.

I should like to kill both of you today.

For trespassing is a sin I must say."

P L A T O

"Step back or I will hit you with a leek.

I can blind you with my weapon so sleek.

Or, run when you laugh so hard that you fall.

If you have help, now is the time to call."

I B E F I X

"That is not how you kill such an old witch.

Garlic on your points will make her soon twitch.

Grind her spine in a mortar and pestle.

Then, she will be hot, ready to wrestle."

D E B

"You three are so worthless and very lame.

I wanted to have a laugh just the same.

I will not appear as a savage beast.

Let us now relax and enjoy this feast."

Ibefix Joins the Group on the Trade Route from Narbo and Massalia
Founded by the Phocaean Greeks in Southern Gaul to Alalia
a Corsu-Phocaean Greek City in Eastern Corsica Named for Al and Alia

IBEFIX

"I know each of you, but not all know me.

 You are here as Phocis crossed the sea.

Greek and Corsu are one in a coast port.

Gaul's wine goes east for dye and the sort."

AL

"Phocis makes the path the Sherden once made.

West to the Ebro where olive trees make shade.

East to Cor's cave where grapes now make wine.

Southeast below Cor's cove the plain is fine."

DEB

"I knew your parents fighting on the wall.

They came east to rear you when you small.

You run the town Phocis named for you.

To hold the trade route for only a few."

PLATO

"The tribes are absent from the sandy plain.

A marble temple glistens in the rain.

The agora sells ideas and fresh food.

Greek hubris and local pride are good."

ALIA

"I sense what we have my not last so long.

Birds see purple sails and forget their song.

I know that logic is our true path.

Thus, greed for all trade may soon bring us wrath."

Pascal Paul Piazza
**Queen Dido of Carthage and Descendent of Volpe and Cyrene and Arch-Antagonist
to Cor and Sica's Heirs and Luli the Carthaginian Admiral
Marshal Troops from Throughout North Africa**

DIDO

"I want all my subjects to raise the host.

There are sixty empty ships on the coast.

Each to be filled with fifty on the oars.

And fifty spears make each boat look like boars."

LULI

"Our men are ready and wanting to fight.

They are steeled to show off their firm might.

Trained with javelin, shield, sword and bow.

Prepared to watch over those who row."

DIDO

"Prygi joins us with sixty of his own.

It will be a display of fealty shown.

But, our men will be the best sailing crews.

Boarding boats so that we cannot lose."

LULI

"There are many who march under our flag.

There is no will so their courage may lag.

Horsemen on foot wonder why they are there.

Pirates stroke oars with pain, fear and despair."

DIDO

"Did I not give them each a choice to make?

Do they now think they made a mistake?

I decree it, that ends it, what else to say.

The oar pits will give them their time to pray."

**Numid the Numidian and Hanno the Berber Contemplate the Meaning of Service
in the Carthaginian Navy or Army as Federate Troops**

NUMID

"Why do we all accept the purple flag?

Flying over each beach, mountain and crag?

Our tribes seek much more than the purple dye.

Robust rulers ride on the dessert dry."

HANNO

"I am Hanno, but a Berber by birth.

The Atlas is home and source of my worth.

We are a small group alert and alive.

So, we provide troops just to survive."

NUMID

"The horse is in us and we are the horse.

We strike light lighting in the truest course.

Dido came from all sides aiming to kill.

With one purpose of our fresh blood to spill."

HANNO

"We are raiders who met them long ago.

We gave in and went where the winds did blow.

I got my name from their king of the sails.

Now we choose between either troops or jails."

NUMID

"Do we reason with her to restore hope?

Or, do we hang at the end of a rope?

Who is this queen alone in her palace?

Does she rule with wisdom or pure malice?"

HANNO

"Dido founded Carthage to stoke her fire.
It was why she abandoned all with Tyre.
She burned with the flames of one sole end.
She was on a set path that did not bend."

NUMID

"She had to found a city that was great.
Her wit, charm and face left no other fate.
She could lead like no one else thought to lead.
She could argue as no one else could plead".

HANNO

"She was lean and tall with a runner's grace.
Her age and toil did not show on her face.
She could lure God or mortal with a glance.
Her beauty caught everyone in a trance."

NUMID

"She won with her wry wit and active mind.
Her path was certain and not hard to find.
She could answer what no one knew to ask.
She would do what nobody sought to task."

HANNO

"Yet, she was known more for her black bile.
To destroy Cyrnos was more than her trial.
From Volpe, she received magma hot hate.
From Cyrene, envy became her sole fate."

Numid and Hanno Meet with Narsu the Corsican Traitor Who Seeks and Receives an Audience with Queen Dido

NUMID

"Do you come to meet with Dido who reigns?

Do you have the tact, the wits or the brains?

You do not have her skill to hunt or fight.

You will be cast aside in the dark night."

NARSU

"I am Narsu and I seek the young queen.

I seek my cousin whom I have not seen.

Where is she who rules with pure Punic pride?

Who is supreme over both land and tide?"

HANNO

"She has no family of whom we know.

She will not listen to some magic show.

She only cares to prepare for the war.

Which she soon will bring forth from this old shore."

NARSU

"That is why she will see me right away.

She will want to hear what I have to say.

I have a plan to make sure she will win.

She will have revenge on her long lost kin."

NUMID

"Good luck, we have waited for many days.

We have been told to leave in many ways.

We cannot fight as she asks us to do.

We are not fodder to serve as a crew."

DIDO

"Who claims to be of my pure goddess blood?

Yet, looks like a peasant covered in mud?

But, my compassion exudes no known bounds.

Your words best be like sweet choral sounds."

NARSU

"You want to draw Phocis out in the sea.

You want him to sail his ships against me.

Then your vise can crack him like a nut.

Your strike will be like a mortal knife cut."

DIDO

"I hear a bell clang making noise aloud.

Your words are translucent like a cloud.

If Phocis dies, then Cyrnos will be mine.

You have said why he will act like kine."

NARSU

"I come from the island that you so hate.

I know Alia that they love so great.

I will kidnap her and sail to your coast.

Phocis will not resist to stop my boast."

DIDO

"How do I know that it is not a trap?

That you do not lead me into his lap?

You are way too sharp to double-cross me.

Take those two and start a war on the sea."

**The Phocaean Greeks Swell the Population of Alalia with Refugees from
Their Burnt Home in Asia Minor While Prygi the Etruscan Fumes
that More Greeks Hurt Their Trade Empire**

ALIA

"Laughter rose in the agora today.

Sales were brisk of foreign foods in each bay.

Debates were fierce without any true end.

But civic life is a cure that does mend."

AL

"Phocis knew more when he told you to stay.

Corsu and Greeks meld in a special way.

Your numbers though increase by the day.

More ships than at Cor's cave or Narbo bay."

PLATO

"Yes, we all come as our home is on fire.

The Persian torch builds flames ever higher.

Our temple invites all now to arrive.

It is here first that we will all survive."

IBEFIX

"We are a picture of different hues.

There are Ubil, Pict and Parisi crews.

Aedui and Etrusci sell and brag.

There is even room for the purple flag."

ALIA

"The augur tells us that Prygi fumes.

Left undone only bloodshed and war looms.

You three must sail to calm his temper down.

I stay to meet Narsu and show him our town."

Alia Meets with Narsu, Numid and Hanno and is Kidnapped

A L

"He is where the Numidian is found.

Next to the Berber's red tent on the ground.

We must leave as we have no time to waste.

Give him praise and fine wine and food to taste."

A L I A

"Welcome horseman to our home and our port.

And to your Berber friend far from his fort.

Is this your fine tent where Narsu does sit?

I hope you have time to relax a bit."

N U M I D

"It is true there is no finer host than you.

This could be my home if the wind blew true.

I have no wax, pitch or honey on me.

Your long lost friend is in the tent to see."

N A R S U

"You are wealth beyond our small humble tent.

You bestow such favor that is god-sent.

I know seeing me now is a great shock.

Come in off the jetty from the wet rock."

A L I A

"Hug me as the prodigal has come back.

You act as if I am set to attack.

Let us feast 'til dawn as you are my guest.

I offer you wine and lamb at their best."

N A R S U

"I fear my time is short and cannot change.

I must meet some ships within a close range.

I have to bring a gift wrapped up tight.

I need your help and all of my might."

A L I A

"You speak in riddles, but can I assist.

I must help you, as I cannot resist.

What is it that you ask me now to do?

I am not a kitten learning to mew!"

H A N N O

"Get out right now or face a certain fate.

You will each die if you hector or wait.

The port is ablaze with hot naphtha heat.

Jump into our ship and off of your feet."

A L I A

"I cannot retreat and leave my port to burn.

I must direct the town's very turn.

I can swim under water with no sound.

Soon, I dive and will be firmly on the ground."

N A R S U

"Gather her quickly in her prison net.

Keep her wrapped up like a new prize pet.

I knew she would dive and get herself caught.

Dido closely seeks the gift that she bought."

Queen Dido Received Alia Onboard the Carthaginian Flagship

DIDO

"I wear the armor that Deb gave away.

I tricked Deb to be under my sway.

She did not know the words I used on her.

I prayed the first words of the magic cur."

ALIA

"Yet, you tie me up in a wet net this day.

Prancing, boasting and crowing in your way.

Face me with some honor lance upon lance.

Let me go and give me a single chance."

DIDO

"I outwit Deb so I do not fear you.

I am immune even if your aim is true.

I will draw out the Greeks with you as bait.

We will keep all our ships in line and wait."

ALIA

"We will soon fight on that I have no doubt.

It is not long before I draw you out.

Your hot hate drives you so you do not think.

You have wrongly brought the world to the brink."

DIDO

"Your brother will face twice as many ships.

I will relish how my sword cuts and rips.

With yours and his blood staining the Great Sea.

Cor and Sica's heirs will succumb to me."

A Talking Honey Badger Visits Alia Tied Up in a Cargo Hold on the Carthaginian Flagship

TALKING HONEY BADGER

"It is so dank and damp here my fur reeks.

You may not know such a badger that speaks.

I have come now to lift your spirits here.

Your brother and Ibefix soon should be near."

ALIA

"Wow, I guess a lion was not around.

Or an eagle as it makes too much sound.

How can you help me when she won before?

She cannot be hurt to even the score."

TALKING HONEY BADGER

"I can be a fish that swims far from here.

So you stay tied up alone in fear.

Hubris made her miss key words of making.

I let her win to be ripe for the taking."

ALIA

"Will I get the chance to face off with her?

My mind is keen and my blood will soon stir.

I have a javelin that bears her name.

I will not do it for profit or fame."

TALKING HONEY BADGER

"You will fight as that is the goal of fate.

Sixty ships arrive and thus you must wait.

Take the fleece you wear and the oil I spray.

You will lead the men and win the day."

***The Phocaean Greeks Phocis, Plato, Papalas and Ajax, Al and Ibefix
Learn of the Abduction of Alia and Plan a Rescue and Attack on Queen Dido
Thinking the Prygi and the Etruscans Will Not Join Queen Dido***

AL

"Phocis, we are glad to see you this day.

We have good news Pyrgi remains at bay.

He was angry and hurt but could be bought.

A better trade deal is what he had sought."

PHOCIS

"By Zeus, it is true that you do not know.

Narsu took Alia to please Dido.

I saw this coming, but not in this way.

We will have sixty ships to sail this day."

AJAX

"We had sources who provide us with tips.

Dido has been rabidly building ships.

She ordered all tribes to supply her crews.

That she is ready to strike is not news."

PAPALAS

"In covert coves we designed a new fleet.

And a battle plan both new and discrete.

We will first wield a weapon waging war.

A Gaulish bronze ram will even the score."

PLATO

"We sail like we did for Helen of old.

With less ships tho' than what Homer told.

The reasons we sail are one in the same.

We seek honor, respect, revenge and fame."

**The Corsu-Greek Order of Battle: Sixty Pentercounters Outfitted
with the Naval Innovation of the Battering Ram and a New Tactic
Not to Fight Side-By-Side in Rows**

PHOCIS

"Each pentercounter projects pride and strength.

Fourteen feet wide and sixty feet in length.

Fifty oars match eighty of hoplite class.

A brazen bronze ram breaks ship beams like glass."

PAPALAS

"Six rows of ten form an ancient array.

They must think we will fight in this old way

But, we will draw them out not side-by-side.

Sinking each ship so they drown in the tide."

PLATO

"The oars stroke singing in rhythm and pace.

They know that it is to death they race.

Javelins are sharp and bows are strung tight.

Hoplites raise sword and shield to show their might."

AL

"The sea is calm unlike the hearts that beat.

The sun is warm forming sweat in the heat.

The sight is clear leaving all in plain view.

The steel is set freezing eyes of the crew."

IBEFIX

"We come to help Corsu and Greek as one.

Our lives are at stake 'til the work is done

We are free not subjects far from our home.

Where we will return to Spain, Gaul and Rome."

Pascal Paul Piazza

**The Carthaginian-Etruscan Order of Battle: One Hundred Twenty Ships
with the Etruscans Deployed to the Port and the Carthaginians Deployed
to the Bow of the Corsu-Greek Navy in Straight Rows**

DIDO

"Phocis sails into a sure trap so wise.

Twenty ships to his port setting the vise.

Ten lines of ten just waiting to deploy.

Our side-by-side attack is the true ploy."

LULI

"You have chosen well the place of battle.

The waves will shake making the earth rattle.

They must advance with no port to retreat.

I need no bird spleen to augur their defeat."

DIDO

"I create fate as if the die is cast.

The troops look ready from first to last.

Side-by-side we will shock the hoplite host.

It will be Greek blood that erupts the most."

LULI

"I will trust each cone helmet and round shield.

That takes from the Sun its glare as its yield.

Perfect order and spears display our great might.

They will die from fright before trying to fight."

DIDO

"Purple and turquoise will prevail this day.

Bards will long speak of what happens today.

Start the troop chant of how great I will be.

Once we win this true battle on the sea."

The Battle of Alalia – Phase One
Corse-Gaulish Ships Draw Out the Etruscans Under Admiral Agyalla
and Ram Individual Ships with No Side-By-Side Engagements

A L

"Phocis is through with forty in four rows.

Baiting the Etruscans to see what shows.

He likes his odds if he can draw them out.

He is outnumbered if they turn about."

A G Y A L L A

"This is a dilemma as we now start.

Moving south poses a spear to my heart.

Going straight west puts the sun in their face.

We thus attack side-by-side at our pace."

I B E F I X

"Invite them to fight man-to-man on decks.

They will soon learn our goal is to make wrecks.

They do not know what for them is in store.

We are about to start a new kind of war."

A G Y A L L A

"Ready the archers and the rope lines to throw.

They will soon receive a gift from our bows.

But wait, they break line following no path.

Each ship find a ship to bestow your wrath."

P A P A L A S

"Perfect, find a ship to ram in the stern.

Beams will break starting to twist and to turn

They will have to swim rather than to fight.

Bows and spears will not overcome their fright."

Pascal Paul Piazza

The Resulting Destruction of the Etruscan Force is Complete.
The Etruscans and Their Berber and Numidian Federate Troops are Offered Generous Terms

AGYALLA

"I know that I did everything I was told.

Yet, my men die submerged in water so cold.

They never could shoot or strike with such force.

Eighteen ships lost as a matter of course."

AL

"You can keep your ship if your men stand down.

You can save your men and not let them drown.

They and you were brave and worthy to fight.

But, you must withdraw before we lose light."

AGYALLA

"We can leave and not become your new slaves!

Say we lost to new tactics on the waves.

I do not think Dido will do the same.

Your deeds today will surely add to your fame."

IBEFIX

"The last ship may leave as Numid I know.

Berber and horsemen are not now our foe.

We may fight one day to protect our home.

From some other tribe that chooses to roam."

NUMID

"I never thought that ships could so fall.

To owe a debt to some Corsu or Gaul.

We thank you my friends and so do our wives.

We prefer to leave and not have lost lives."

The Battle of Alalia – Phase Two
Greek and Corse-Gaulish Ships Engage the Carthaginians and the Remaining Etruscans

PHOCIS

"The odds are closer having won this morn.

She still has more ships fueled by hate and scorn.

She will not know the tactics we used well.

So, break the lines as if under a spell."

LULI

"What sorcery is this breaking the lines?

Do they run and hide afraid of the signs?

Hunt them down one-by-one now if we must.

It is our force and numbers that I trust."

PLATO

"The ramming had the same result at first.

Forty more crews lost when the beams burst.

The rams crushed wood so lashed and sewn.

It split and fractured like rock on a bone."

LULI

"We wait the next ram on forty more.

To see if Phocis can even the score.

Our hubris must give way to simple luck.

By Ba'al the last rams only got stuck."

AJAX

"Eighty boats linked is the field of war.

Hand-to-hand combat saw the death toll soar.

Heroes had not lost such blood and sinew.

Eighty ships lost and most of each crew."

During the Side-By-Side Fighting Alia Set Lose by Deb Duels with Queen Dido

D I D O

"I will not lose if I must kill them all.

None of them can hurt me or make me fall.

I did what Tyre decided not to do.

An impasse is not a result too true."

A L I A

"You think of you when your men so suffer.

They bleed and grasp air seeking a buffer.

They feel they will be slaves or something worse.

It is your name they all will soon curse."

D I D O

"You smell like a rodent my dogs would kill.

It does not matter your blood will spill.

You must fight me and on that I agree.

Feel the point of my spear cut you in three."

A L I A

"Your spear splits like the stern of a boat.

You should learn to listen before you gloat.

Deb gave you the armor with one main flaw.

It fears iron from the forge of the law."

D I D O

"I brought cities to your tribes at one time.

I am repaid with such riddles and rhyme.

Throw your spear and see if I bleed red.

I get your one point as now I am dead."

The Aftermath of the Battle of Alalia

P H O C I S

"This is a sad Cadmeian win of course.

We have gladness tempered with remorse.

Alia is back and Dido is dead.

The Styx flows with too much blood so red."

P L A T O

"We will re-group to the south-east of here.

We take our twenty ships and most Greeks there.

Massalia and Narbo are still ports.

Waiting for the Etrusci and like sorts."

A L

"We stand on deals with the Etrusci made.

We will move them when we trade.

We will sell much wax, pitch and honey.

We welcome Troy's sons and all their money."

A L I A

"Punic pride did not die much less subside.

They will be kings of the most southern tide.

They are welcome here to trade and to buy.

If they do what Tyre long sought to try."

I B E F I X

"The tribes of this isle stay beyond the fray.

My tribes though have to be right in the way.

The Ebro to Cor's cave makes a ripe path.

I fear it will be the source of great wrath."

CHAPTER THIRTEEN

CELTS/GAULS

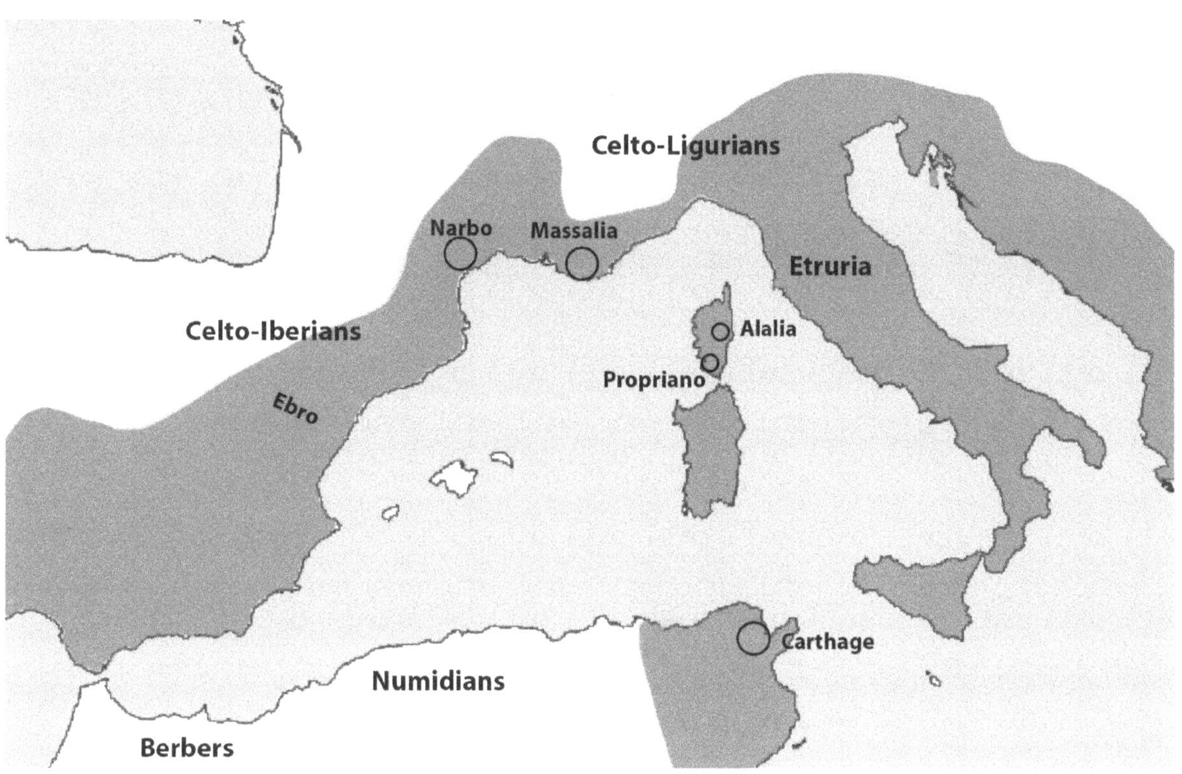

Roman Republic of 52 BCE

Roman-Gaul – 491 CE

The Roman Quintet: What is Old is New Again
The Siege of Alesia September 52 BCE to Seneca's Exile 40 CE

HYPERBOLIUM

"The heirs of Troy would not be held back.

Mother wolf's milk put them on the right track.

It left the shadow of a tyrant's heels.

The people's senate then ruled seven hills."

DELIRIUM

"Rome absorbed all of the tribes on the boot.

While civics, rhetoric and law took root.

It saw what it liked beyond the Alps.

'Til the Gauls hit back and took a few scalps."

PESSIMISSIUM

"Carthage and Rome were rivals from the start.

When neither could keep the sea trade apart.

Rome won three wars that were long and hard fought.

It sought new land with the peace that it bought."

MARY

"Rome won Corsica with the first won war.

Southern Gaul came next opening the door.

The other three parts came after a hard siege.

When Gaul paid homage to Rome as its liege."

CHARLOTTE

"Rome became an empire of force and thought.

Put to the sure test that could not be bought.

Foederates were Rome until they were not.

Then Rome was new Rome by a Papal plot."

Pascal Paul Piazza
**Ursufix the Descendent of Alia and Ibefix Fights with Vercingetorix
and the Gauls During the Siege of Alesia by Julius Caesar
Who Has Encircled Alesia with a Fortified Trench While being Encircled Himself**

DEB

"I would like to be in Brandu alone.

 Swimming, sleeping and smelling a pine cone.

Why am I on a hill in northeast Gaul?

Under siege by Caesar in the cold Fall?"

URSUFIX

"We fight the Romans with a single chief.

Gauls gather to provide us with relief.

One Gaul united we surpass the odds.

With the same spirit we defy the gods."

DEB

"Romans form a circle around a hill.

Caesar is ruthless and ready to kill.

Gauls attack from the inside and beyond.

It is bad and I have no magic wand."

URSUFIX

"You have no magic that we need.

Our land and our hope is our true seed.

Ibefix and Alia are my kin.

I am very certain that we will win."

DEB

"I knew them six hundred years in the past.

I see that their spirit lives and did last.

Your ruler has given up so you may live.

That is smart for you have a lot to give."

**300 Corsicans are Made a Foederate Numerus
After the Surrender of Vercingetorix at Alesia Based Upon
the Reputation Acquired in the Roman-Corsican Wars of 262-161 BCE**

FABIAN MAXIMUS - PRIMU PILUS LEGIO XIII GEMINA

"The treaty with the Gauls contains a prize.

Three hundred whose line makes our valor rise.

All twelve tribes are now present in our ranks.

In your battles you will give the gods thanks."

FLAVIUS MAXIMUM - CENTURION LEGIO XIII GEMINA

"It took one hundred years to win their land.

They let us find peace on their terms in hand.

We won the coast, the cities and the wheat.

They held the maquis knowing we were beat."

FABIAN MAXIMUS - PRIMU PILUS LEGIO XIII GEMINA

"Scipio burnt the Punic port with fire.

He kept fighting as the ground was higher.

He had never faced a stronger foe.

He won, but at what price did he show."

FLAVIUS MAXIMUM - CENTURION LEGIO XIII GEMINA

"Claudius beat them, but his terms were fair. V

arus was mad and sent him to their lair.

Hoping the tribes would kill a Roman now.

Yet, he returned unharmed and with a cow."

FABIAN MAXIMUS - PRIMU PILUS LEGIO XIII GEMINA

"Many died on both sides in the Myrtle Field.

A mountain home still made Caius have to yield.

Death and wax tribute did not make them stop.

Ten more years and they had their mountain top."

FLAVIUS MAXIMUM - CENTURION LEGIO XIII GEMINA

"Behold the strength of Jupiter and Mars.

Made flesh in the man blessed by the stars.

Who women want and lions hide from shame.

You now are near to the eternal flame."

FLAVIUS MAXIMUM - CENTURION LEGIO XIII GEMINA

"This long war ends with a well-earned pact.

Displaying Caesar's guile and clever tact.

This numerus is your new hearth and home.

Honor the senate and people of Rome."

FLACCUS OPTIO

"We won the war but I am stuck with you.

Three hundred Corsu allied as a zoo.

You each lie, cheat, rape and defile our faith.

You will hover around me like a wraith."

URSUFIX

"We are Corsu and fought for all of Gaul.

We are proud even if our king did fall.

Why do you defame us without a chance?

We beat you once like you were in a trance."

FLACCUS OPTIO

"All of that did not seem much to matter.

They gave you to us as they get fatter.

You are Romans now within a strange game.

You will be Murus for your new name."

Maurus Trains as a Tirones (New Recruit)

FLACCUS OPTIO

"The gladius is our power and might.

It is deadly in a hand-to-hand fight.

Just its sight has caused men to withdraw.

You thrust like spear not slash like a saw."

MURUS

"It is not the sword that makes you so cruel.

It is not the long trails or the cold gruel.

It is the lust to punish with a point.

The praise to rend flesh and to cut a joint."

FLACCUS OPTIO

"The shield is your roof when arrows will fall.

Locked as one it makes a seamless wall.

A horse is too smart to charge, but not men.

The shield hides a sharp sword to thrust again."

MURUS

"Mettle not metal should be your true force.

Wit and not routine should set the right course.

A shield should be light to move all around.

Not fixed and rigid tied to the ground."

FLACCUS OPTIO

"I live beyond my first twenty-five term.

My sweat and blood cover many a berm.

The skills I teach are why I am here now.

And not bone meal for some boar or old cow."

Maurus Faces Battle in Spain

FLACCUS OPTIO

"You have long trained, but this morn we fight.

Are you ready to draw blood at first sight?

Are you afraid to die so you will run?

Pray to your gods with the rays of the Sun."

MAURUS

"We are the spirit of the standing stones.

Destiny is that and the Evil Eye hones.

Honor as one will show us the true way.

We will do battle and win on this day."

FLACCUS OPTIO

"We will be on the legion's far right side.

We will be alone as we march out wide.

The tribes of the Ebro are fierce and good.

Waiting for us among the stone and wood."

MAURUS

"The Ebro has always been a safe place.

Goods went west with tribes filling open space.

Before we were on a different path.

We welcome the full bull brunt of their wrath."

FLACCUS OPTIO

"Men, cover and form a square that is tight.

Face them all around with spears in plain sight.

Absorb all blunt blows, stones, spears, swords and more.

Our valor will be part of our true lore."

FLACCUS OPTIO

"Four strong sorties fell to our metal wall.

Their pulse is weak, as they all soon will fall.

Draw swords so that we bring this to an end.

Cut off a hand as the message we send."

MAURUS

"You call us savage in our tribal rites?

We have won the field staying on the heights.

They are nowhere to be seen or to fight.

Let us mark the valor with colors bright."

FLACCUS OPTIO

"Our foes return if you do not rend flesh.

Power is force and not a moral mesh.

Our order was strong to my great surprise.

I felt your tribes would leave or try to reprise."

MAURUS

"Honor binds us where blood is not the same.

We owe the land and not a quest for fame.

Out acts bond us to Rome and its glory.

But, we are our island and its story."

FLAVIUS MAXIMUS

"The legion won because you did not yield.

Three thousand have run from your sword and shield.

The revolt is over, as is this war.

I bestow now the order of the boar."

Pascal Paul Piazza

The Corsican Numerus Earns the Baton of the Boar and Become Road Builders

FLACCUS OPTIO

"I guess that your kind are all like the boar.

We thought that such a name makes your heart soar.

Let us drink wine before we return to Gaul.

We have cities and roads to build for all."

FORTIS

"The boar is who we are and who we should be.

It is a totem that we all can see.

But, now we will not fight, but will lay bricks?

I do not work well with mud, straw and sticks."

FLACCUS OPTIO

"Our built roads and bridges make us move fast.

Crossing rivers when the die is so cast.

The German thought the Rhine could not be beat.

Their mistake led to their own quick defeat."

FLACCUS OPTIO

"We make cities where did Celt, Greek and Gaul.

Places to live even after Rome may fall.

For a thousand or more years the forum is laid.

Whomever lives there will live off the trade."

MAURUS

"Making the land peaceful is a smart thing.

One could live well of the wealth it brings.

Troops may be sent to conquer other land.

Marble may stand for a leader so grand."

FLACCUS OPTIO

"There are five layers to any Roman way.

Level and ram the ground tight as I say.

Next, lay rough-hewn stones the size of my hand.

Then, rough and fine concrete in layers grand."

FLACCUS OPTIO

"Then top it off with concave surface stones.

Edged on both sides with rocks that break bones.

We will dig a hole as deep as Maurus is tall.

And as wide as if Maurus were to fall."

FORTIS

"How will we know where and how far to dig.

We have built hills with forts that were big.

But, we have not dug down to build a road.

Or, built something for public use by code."

MAURUS

"What is this concrete and how is it made?

How do you pour it to meet the right grade?

Are we making a road or digging my grave?

Is this how we will show that we are brave?"

FLACCUS OPTIO

"You will dig and that is all you need know.

Strings will be set for you all to follow.

The Immunes will direct the whole scene.

Telling you what to pick up and to screen."

Pascal Paul Piazza

**Maurus and the Corsicans Are Punished for Not Telling on a Fellow Corsican
When the Roman Civil War Erupts and They Join Julius Caesar to Cross the Rubicon
Which They are Forbidden to Do**

FORTIS

"Five moons have gone and the road is all done.

We feel like we all went to war and won.

We now can leave more quickly and go home.

You can leave us and return back to Rome."

MAURUS

"There were few problems to get to this point.

Every ten of us were whipped at each joint.

We would not tell who took the Roman bell.

Even if you know, you still do not tell."

FLACCUS OPTIO

"I do not understand this tribal code.

But, I welcome your work and the new road.

Civil war reigns and we must take our flight.

Going to Rome quickly to show off our might."

MAURUS

"You ask why our tribes so often will fight.

I would ask you the same this very night.

Does not the law forbid our path to Rome?

Are we all not outlaws far from our home?"

FLACCUS OPTIO

"The Rubicon is just water to pass.

I take my orders from the ruling class.

Caesar will oust Pompey and his cohorts.

Tracking them down to cities and to forts."

Julius Caesar Follows His Only Rival and the Elder General Pompey to Pharsalus in Greece to End the Civil War, But Pompey Deploys Some Tactical Tricks Before Losing the Baton of the Boar

MAURUS

"We have now gone from Gaul to Rome to Greece.

We take a path like Jason and the fleece.

We do not seek magic, but an old man.

Who will soon fight on his ground if he can."

FORTIS

"Pompey has his allies on the quick march.

We stay put like we were tied to some arch.

Are we bait bringing their troops in the clear?

I feel a ghostly heart beat and breath near."

MAURUS

"We must move based upon what we see.

We should send up a young scout in a tree.

Yet, men raise your shields preparing for war.

We now defend the baton of the boar."

FLACCUS OPTIO

"Pull back, it is an ambush from the start.

Your retreat is now blocked by a cart.

But, they will not kill any of my men.

I will rush them even at one-on-ten."

FORTIS

"Has he lost his mind as well as his life?

Has this civil war created too much strife?

But, we know that he acts for our good health.

Let us march forward now and quit this stealth."

MAURUS

"Gladius set, we march in good order.

We will push these foes across the border.

A boar does not back down or feign retreat.

It draws blood and flesh without a defeat."

FORTIS

"Charge fast now and we will have no regrets.

Sing our hymn with nothing left to forget.

Surround Flaccus now as soon as we can.

We will die if we must to the last man."

MAURUS

"I have found him so our oath has been met.

Back scum, this is one that they will not get.

Fight me as I stand and fight in one place.

I am ready to meet you face to face."

FORTIS

"We have him now and he can fully stand.

But, he did break some ribs and his left hand.

We follow Mars who today is reborn.

Ready to reap defeat on top of scorn."

MAURUS

"Our baton is high to be seen by all.

Fueled by honor we cannot fall.

Roman fights Roman in a tribal fight.

Fealty to duty supplies us our might."

FLACCUS OPTIO

"Why do we wait making them pay right now?

They are old and fat like a dower sow.

This boar cannot be stopped when it acts.

Destiny cannot overcome these facts."

FORTIS AND MAURUS

"String the colors and let out a brash roar.

Faster and faster you beautiful boar.

We want to hold their standard in our hand.

Crush their fasces in pieces on the sand."

FLACCUS OPTIO

"They ran like rodents when they saw us come.

Pompey left knowing he could not overcome.

The standard belongs to our men so brave.

The end of each battle is what we crave."

MAURUS

"You saved us as if you might really care

To die for some savages if you dare.

There is but one unit with its own name.

With a balding leader that has no shame."

FLAVIUS MAXIMUS

"Pharsalus was won by your steadfast deeds.

Caesar wants to care for all of your needs.

Pompey runs fast, but soon he will be caught.

Your unit goes home because how you fought."

Pascal Paul Piazza

The Corsican Boar Numerus is Deployed Home
to Aleria as a Reward for Supporting the Successful Campaign of Julius Caesar

FORTIS

"I will be home when the maquis smells sweet.

Back in my village with women to greet.

Not in some Roman town set on the coast.

I hope that I can find a good boar roast."

MAURUS

"This was a Corsu town when Rome was small.

This should be an old home for one and all.

Rome won it all in the first Punic war.

It changed the name, but not the true core."

FORTIS

"Your kin are from here so you will feel free.

I need rams, foxes and a chestnut tree.

The others seek standing stones and the west.

Ajax's town and women they deem best."

FLACCUS OPTIO

"You could be in Egypt lost in the East.

Left to the intrigue of the young queen's feast

Where a gift was Pompey's severed head.

Chances are that now we would all be dead."

MAURUS

"We are here to build, which is Rome's true grace.

To find the best of Rome and our great race.

We served with pride, faith and honor too.

We should get all things from Rome that is due."

The Building Projects 48-44 BCE

FLACCUS OPTIO

"Caesar sends us money to build his name.

All should know his bounty and his true fame.

We will build a circus with his figure tall.

And, a temple to Diana for all."

MAURUS

"We have marble quarries in the ground.

But, so few roads for us to get around.

Kill or take a donkey will start a war.

That will persist for long decades or more."

FLACCUS OPTIO

"I will not let some tribal rite take hold.

If I must, I will takes all measures bold.

The wheat and trade need a road for the sale.

We will make your bread from wheat by the bale."

MAURUS

"All roads across the sea may lead to Rome.

All roads here start and return to my home.

Staring from Aleria and then back.

They will stick to the coast free from attack."

FLACCUS OPTIO

"Sulla's dull camp must shine with Caesar's name.

Mariana's marble must shout his fame.

Then to Meria with concrete so fine.

Moving bundles of wheat and casks of wine."

Pascal Paul Piazza

The Road is Finished on the Ides of March When the Hubris of Power is Checked and the Glory of Building is Reaffirmed

MAURUS

"Four years have gone and the road is near done.

It should be complete by the next ten Suns.

Wheat will grow along the way to make bread.

Ground at circle mills made of stone and lead."

FORTIS

"It is the Ides of March with omens bad.

Clouds provide a cloak for the Sun is sad.

We break our backs without getting ahead.

Only you labor for your past words said."

MAURUS

"Yes, I work as I freely gave my word.

After the Gauls sold me like an old bird.

We can build the Roman dream we need.

It is not the fasces for which we bleed."

FLACCUS OPTIO

"The month of March ends and our task is done.

This is just one more battle that we won.

Things though are unknown as Caesar is dead.

Brutus has turned the Senate floor red."

MAURUS

"Caesar was too big so he had to fall.

He heard the wrong words making a bad call.

Brutus had honor doing what is right.

Who now pays us to build roads or fight?"

FLACCUS OPTIO

"The civil war will be fought in the east.

Caesar's heir needs wheat and honey to feast. Money comes to keep us on our own path.

Bread is the bribe quelling the plebian wrath."

FORTIS

"Octavian thus makes the people cheer.

Like babies blind to own chains and fear.

He is Apollo resplendent in light.

Far from the sinew torn in the blood fight."

MAURUS

"Do we think that peace is such a bad fate?

Do we mark this day as an evil date?

We no longer build for Caesar's late fame.

We will build without saying our true name."

FORTIS

"We have three hundred men ready to fight

Rome is open to fall to our true might.

No geese will call to reveal our attack.

It will cost them much to get their Rome back."

FLACCUS OPTIO

"Such hubris fuels us to make the mock charge.

To dream of glory on the field writ large.

But not to find out the blood to be lost.

When two legions attack us at all cost."

Pascal Paul Piazza
***The Civil War and the Roman Republic End with Octavian Declaring Himself
Emperor Caesar Augustus and Fortis and Maurus Being
Released From Service - 27 BCE***

FORTIS

"After all these years do you have no guilt?

Scarring our old coast with what he has built.

Concrete and stone kill the woods of our name.

Corsa's bull will not come here just the same."

MAURUS

"The forum laughs with a speaker's quick quip.

Goods from the Pontus come with the next ship.

A Mihtric temple paints the path east.

Flour finds a path on roads for a feast."

FORTIS

"These are for Rome and not the local tribes.

They care not for drama or for new scribes.

They smell the maquis watching from on high.

What is on the ground is not in the sky."

MAURUS

"I love the tribes, but there has to be more.

Babu built cities and texts in the lore.

Chord pots from the north met stones from the south.

Our tradition is passed by word of mouth."

FORTIS

"Phocis and the Sherden came here to trade.

They built some ports not temples on the grade.

Now the coast is a grape ripe on the vine.

Inviting conquest drinking some new wine."

FLACCUS OPTIA

"Your twenty-five years of service now ends.

You brothers should go drink and make amends.

You are citizens of Rome on your own.

Free to travel where only birds have flown."

FORTIS

"I do not thank you for being a slave.

I am free again now just like a wave.

A feoderate once, but not your ally.

Stay away from where chestnut trees lie."

FLACCUS OPTIA

"We have a bond beyond a tribe or clan.

Two bound like only the fear of death can.

I honor your valor which springs from pride.

We will not venture where you will reside."

MAURUS

"My debt is paid, but I do not leave now.

Where can we all live together and how?

I must know the village and city square.

Facing the wild and the senate in their lair."

DEB

"I was there when the Gauls gave you away.

I, therefore, am here on this special day.

Fortis, go home and return to your past.

Maurus, find a boar to hunt that is fast."

Pascal Paul Piazza

**Maurus Goes to Meria, Learns Both Female Wit and Village Life from Primu,
Has to Defend Himself from Titre Who is Primu's Brother and Finds His Connection
from the Elder Village Woman Healer**

MAURUS

"I look for boar while two eyes hunt for me.

A terrace breaks the trees for me to see.

Fig trees and root plants form very tight lines.

The next terrace holds green grapes among vines."

MAURUS

"In battle, I would not walk down the path.

Where my foe drives me to focus all wrath.

I crawl with the plants with the Sun so bright.

Face to face with two tusks so old and white."

MAURUS

"With a sharp crack, a branch breaks as we roll.

Tusk and teeth tear and torque taking a toll.

I give as good as I get with my knife.

My blood pulses and pours taking its life."

PRIMU

"Why do you pour your blood over our land?

How can you kill our boar with your own hand?

You should die, as our honor deems it so.

Both dead bodies will so help the crops grow."

MAURUS

"Will you help or must I die to please fate?

Maybe you can find for me some cold slate?

Rend your shirt to stop the flow of my blood.

Soon you will not be able to stop the flood."

PRIMU

"You invade and steal and now want me too!
I hide my breast and arm from one like you.
But, my fun ends, as you are truly hurt.
Please rollover and get out of the dirt."

PRIMU

"Let me clean your wound with water and oil.
I must remove the leaves and all the soil.
This cloth will be tight stopping the blood flow.
This works on my goats as far as I know."

MAURUS

"You goats are lucky to have such kind care.
To be herded by one charming and fair.
I have had some wounds hurt down to my bone.
Nothing would hurt more than being alone."

PRIMU

"I need to treat your leg and not your lust.
You will die unless you give me your trust.
I can apply a balm back in my house.
If you are quiet as would be a mouse."

TITRE

"Such disrespect you scum of Luri show.
You steal my boar and hurt my sister so.
Step back sister and let my dogs go wild.
Chasing him home like a restless child."

PRIMU

"Your advice has been old since I was three.

I can use a knife and take care of me.

My honor is fine, but his leg is not.

He will die if his blood does not soon clot."

TITRE

"Then die he must for he insulted me.

He brings the Evil Eye to our family.

I have killed many men for less than this.

I can only hope that my wound does not miss."

LA DONNA SIGNADORE

"The boar was not yours bearing no such crest.

It was his totem and part of his quest.

Find these herbs and apply them right now.

Stones hum in time telling him not to bow."

TITRE

"He hurt my blood so in it he must drown.

The code is clear that he must be put down.

Or else, my father will haunt me for days.

These are our truth and they are our set ways."

LA DONNA SIGNADORE

"I see the world that you cannot yet see.

Spirits light not to haunt but to help me.

Your zeal is fine but you stopped to look.

What I see from him is an open book."

LA DONNA SIGNADORE

"He shows the conch gifted by the Great Sea.

He is like a star on its course set free.

He is not Luri, but Corsu all good.

He is a tree in that Corsu means wood."

FORTE

"He and I fought for twenty-five long years.

I felt village valor left him like tears.

That he was more than our home could give.

That being Roman is how he should live."

LA DONNA SIGNADORE

"He is like our village ties to the coast.

Allowing us to sit back watching the most.

They still are us but they mix with the rest.

They are the foundation meeting the test."

FORTE

"I am my true name as he is as well.

He is Orsu with truth from an old tale.

Not Gaul or Roman, but how the stones stand.

He is the maquis and strength of our land."

LA DONNA SIGNADORE

"He and Primu were on a path to meet.

Prepare the path for our friends to greet.

Our boar has died so we honor this beast.

We come together to make a great feast."

On the Arrival of Seneca, Nettle the Great Grand-Daughter of Primu and Orsu Appears Before Felix Maximus Who is the Prefect of Aleria – 40 CE

PREFECT FELIX MAXIMUS

"Nettle, my dear, you are too smart to wed.

Yet, your Venus-like shape invites the bed.

Your discourse on Ovid had wit and edge.

Suitors gave up jumping off of the ledge."

NETTLE

"I am born of the edge of village strife.

I know how to cut with words and a knife.

Primu said prefer our honor not looks.

Orsu had us learn the best Roman books."

PREFECT FELIX MAXIMUS

"Virgil, Horace and Ovid all would fear.

Knowing your critique was drawing near.

I must keep Seneca far from you.

He will not like being beaten is true."

NETTLE

"But, that is exactly why I am here.

I so want to challenge his quips and leer.

What better task to speak to the host?

To spar with him to see who learns the most."

PREFECT FELIX MAXIMUS

"You are a citizen and not a slave.

His appetites overcome even the brave.

I will make it so if you so desire.

You have your wish to step into the fire."

Nettle and Seneca

SENECA

"Thugs and animals live all around me.
The gods forsake this place even the sea.
Bring me my nettle branch to strike my back.
Pain lets me forget the culture they lack."

NETTLE

"Do you not mind being thrown in the pack?
Do you not provide the leader they lack?
Here is a nettle branch to pierce your pride.
Your sharp words fall flat listing on your side."

SENECA

"You are well read for a savage and girl.
Disrobe as your skin is soft like a pearl.
I would lead a pack if given the tools.
There is no leader for a group of fools."

NETTLE

"Am I well-read if I have read your books?
Your answer says no as do all your looks.
Cruel lust must have a weakness that I lack.
I suggest that you take a different tack."

SENECA

"You ask that I waste the oil in my krater.
I am happy to act now not later.
No fears or hopes cloud what is before me.
Satisfied with the young whore that I see."

NETTLE

"I should leave as you will have a long night.

Listing the fears you beat in a tough fight.

Embracing new virtue at this first sight.

Your blinders must block out the Sun so bright."

SENECA

"Difficulties enhance the mind like work.

Being in exile, this is my one perk.

This is no moral time beyond this day.

Horace demurs, but it is what I say."

NETTLE

"Things are difficult as you do not dare.

The moment passes as you do not care.

You beat your back because you have no pride.

It is easier just to sit and hide."

SENECA

"I have lost the day for fear of the night.

The night passes for fear of what is right.

I need the quest to meet just those I need.

That is the obvious missing fecund seed."

NETTLE

"Your books tell us to act and overcome fear.

Your acts here show your sloth that is so near.

There are no thugs here but men just like you.

Who lose track when fear guides what we do."

CHAPTER FOURTEEN

Pascal Paul Piazza

The Roman Quintet: The Transition to and the Start of the Early Late Antique World
303 CE – 440 CE

HYPERBOLEUM

"The Late Antique World set the pulse and pace.

The island's foundation is now in place.

Seven hundred years seeds a constant scene.

A coast in flux and a village not seen."

DELERIUM

"A new faith goes from victim to bold king.

Its struggle will find a miter and ring.

Built high by the freedom of village life.

But, fights on doctrine will create great strife."

PESSIMISIUM

"Did Rome in the West witness its own fall?

No, it was transformed both large and small.

Tribes inherited Rome in strength and in pain.

Furs became tunics in search of great gain."

MARY

"Leaders copied generals of past fame.

They copied Latin to win at the game.

Burn and sack some 'til all ears will listen.

'Til the glory of Rome again will glisten."

CHARLOTTE

"Different tribes came and went on the coast.

While villages had many boar to roast.

A town may burn or change its name not trade.

The maquis remained sweet to those unafraid."

Trova (A Descendent of Nettle) Seeks Help from Deb at Brandu

TROVA

"The flame from my torch burns my ashen face.

I look like I lost a close circus race.

I just hope that she can answer my fears.

My family has come here many years."

DEB

"Come, relax, you dour heir of Nettle.

Do not fall, but take my hand and settle.

It has been too long since you were last here.

You look like you need a friend and some cheer."

TROVA

"I do not understand the Roman mind.

Why do they re-write the birth of our kind?

How can Corsu a Trojan be the first?

And Sica, born of Dido, is the worst!"

DEB

"Wow, next time please give me a harder task!

Maybe, what is truth is what you must ask.

Eat some food, as you do know what is true.

They respect you, so they gave birth to you."

TROVA

"They have long sought to take our coastal land.

Their first town before Scipio lies in sand.

Then they burn part and build on the same ground.

They purge hoping we will not be around."

DEB

"They forget the ties that bind them to you.
Time blinds surely as a pigeon will coo.
They listen long to what poets might say.
But, the gladius paved their stone way."

TROVA

"They want our honey, metal, wheat and wax.
Yet, make us provide troops and pay their tax.
Their temple treats us like some feral wave.
Freedom to them means making us a slave."

DEB

"The maquis makes you happy, free and mean.
More equal than they had ever then seen.
They stick to the shore not testing the brave.
They find you too strong to make you a slave."

TROVA

"But, we are an exile for those they now hate.
We are not found to be the gift of fate.
But, there are those of us who seek their way.
They are like pot shards broken in a fray."

DEB

"You are too harsh on them and those around.
They built new cities and the roads on the ground.
The maquis is safe and free to subsist.
Romans and you must and will co-exist."

Deb and Trova Are Approached by a Torch Procession of Roman Legionaries

TROVA

"There are ten flames on the path in a row.

Your tree canopy and stones are aglow.

Should we brace for battle during this night?

I am ready to stand our ground and fight."

FLAVIUS BOREM

"Give us all Christians that you have with you.

They must honor our gods as right and true.

Witch, we know you, but who is this young girl?

Her face and legs are pure like a sea pearl."

DEB

"I should let you find out what she can do.

One against ten though is not fair to you.

How dare you invade my home without care!

Why would we turn over either coarse or fair?"

FLAVIUS BOREM

"We must find the Christian slaves kept from sight.

We must kill more than just this one tonight.

Each slave must honor our old gods or die.

They must affirm that their god is a lie."

TROVA

"Where is the one in chains to give her side?

For Rome, chains make it strong and build its pride.

Yet, one frail woman brings Rome to a knee.

Afraid that her own faith will make her free."

FLAVIUS BOREM

"You impudent cur. I should put chains on you.

Your mouth should be shut for it is not true.

Your die was cast, as you are from coast tribes.

It is not worth even asking for bribes."

GAIUS CRASSUS

"We had been at sea for many long days.

Port was to bring relief in different ways."

Barbarus heard that a girl tried to hide.

A devout young virgin who eschewed pride."

FLAVIUS BOREM

"Her master said her faith was a gift.

Her fealty spread love healing any rift.

Barbarus cried that he did not care.

She must now disrobe letting down her hair."

GAIUS CRASSUS

"She said no defying his cult and his bite.

He had her beaten with rocks at first light.

He broke her mouth and shackled her in chains.

A dove then took her through the crying rains."

DEB

"There is no one here now for you to take.

Leave now for reason and for honor's sake.

You have defiled your gods more than she could.

Take now her path as you know that you should."

A Second Torch Procession of Villagers Dressed in Full Orange Robes with Conical Combined Masks and Hats Approaches Deb and Trovu

T R O V A

"I see dancing orange flames in the full Moon.

I did not think we would have guests this soon.

There are ten in costume from head to toe.

Oil lamp smoke draws spirits in tow."

D E B

"Why do you wear masks and long pointy hats?

You sneak through the night mist like feral cats.

You are no ghosts like I have ever seen.

You invoke no fear, but do make a scene."

E M M A

"We come to rescue any Christians you know.

Romans scavenger like a hungry crow.

Hunting us down if we live our faith.

So, we seek to protect like nighttime wraiths."

L A Z A R U S

"We must hide who we are or we will die.

We raise goats and chestnuts in villages high.

We have no fear, as we walk in His light.

We have a pure mind, as our cause is right."

T R O V A

"When, where and how did you find such belief?

That gives you whole strength and this full relief?

Do you have to wear these orange robes to meet?

Or smear oil on one's face, hands or feet?"

EMMA

"There is more trade than just from Roman ports.

We belong to Gaul's southern sphere of sorts.

It then just came with people as we talked.

It spread in villages as we walked."

LAZARUS

"Christ said we are free and equals as one.

Life is a hard race not easily won.

This is a statement of our village way.

So, this faith now holds a very strong sway."

DEB

"Thus, it may not appear that much was new.

Standing stones become aids for saints so true.

The fabric of a village did not change.

Although our words to use found a new range."

TROVA

"Rome does not know the path that it is on.

The cross should signal for a battle won.

But the cross is an old victim to kill.

This will be more innocent blood to spill."

EMMA

"There is no real need for us to stay here.

This is a place of love and of no fear.

We return to our homes 'til some new day.

Christians can laugh and play among the spray."

The Western Romans Claudius Seneca and Diodorus Debate Taxation of Corsica While News Arrives from Scipio A Week After the Battle of the Milvian Bridge Where Constantine Won Under the Cross - 312 CE

CLAUDIUS SENECA

"Pirates sank the ship with your tax money.

We were left with resin, wax and honey.

That must have been their revenge and plunder.

They will lie and defile the gods' thunder."

DIODORUS

"You know they are stern, but honest and fair.

We burden them taking both foal and mere.

It is cruel the task we impose on them.

And we cut down full stalks both seed and stem."

CLAUDIUS SENECA

"They are ours to do with them how we choose.

If we do not, then it is we who will lose.

They are by nature good slaves to behold.

That is why we keep them within our fold."

DIODORUS

"If we lose them, then we will feel the cost.

First here, then the river buffers are lost.

They are some toy now cast to generals.

To consume all wheat, wood and mineral."

CLAUDIUS SENECA

"Maxentius holds Rome, the Guard and this place.

He must have money to stay in the race.

Constantine will attack to take the crown.

We must tap the ground until it is brown."

DIODORUS

"Rome needs here to live and not to make war.

It needs meat and not the tusk of the boar.

Our troops return with news from Rome this night.

We will now know what occurred in the fight."

SCIPIO

"We were delayed and just saw the battle.

The Guard was cut to pieces like cattle.

They were pinned against the river bank.

The blood flowed over all men and rank."

HORATIO

"Maxentius had destroyed the old stone bridge.

To force the attack to come from the ridge.

Narrow boats would not permit a retreat.

The slaughter was complete from head to feet."

SCIPIO

"I saw something new that chills to the bone.

There was a fervor that set a strong tone.

Each winner's shield displayed a simple cross.

Shouting that "in this" there could be no loss."

HORATIO

"Hold the taxes, as this is a new day.

There are wars to fight in the east they say.

Civil war takes years to restore the peace.

It could take ten years for our pain to cease."

The Cycle of Cyrnos
The Western Roman Diodorus and the New Eastern Roman Prefect Zeno
Debate the Application of the Emperor Constantine's Edict
of Tolerance of 313-314 CE to Corsica - 337 CE

DIODORUS

"Fifteen years have gone since the battle lost.

Today, we learn the true scope of the cost.

A new prefect arrives today from the east.

At least, we can have hope and have a feast."

ZENO

"It is easy to land in this old dock.

I will find the lost taxes on this rock.

Where do I escape this trifling mob?

I need marble and silks to do this job."

DIODORUS

"Salve, my lord, what is to we can do?

What is it will make it easy for you?

We will have food, drink, singing and the dance.

Or, we hear poets or debate on chance."

ZENO

"I want games with death of the cruelest type.

I want Christians to recant all their hype.

I want churches torn down 'til they fall down.

I want their land and to wear my own crown."

DIODORUS

"I cannot possibly do what you ask!

You have given me an illegal task!

If you want me to leave, then I will go.

Just, do not seek to dishonor me so!"

117

ZENO

"I am in charge and cannot break the law.

The law is what I will say and what I saw.

Guard, remove this weak man now from my sight.

I came for wealth, cruelty, and a good fight."

HORATIO

"In the east, the Edict may not be read.

So Christians may be beaten until dead,

Here, the Edict lives in full word and deed.

No one is above this great law and creed."

GLADIUS SUPERBUS

"Constantine knew the Edict was for all.

Each belief is equal and none would fall.

He knew a divided Rome could not stand.

His Council was to unite the whole land."

HORATIO

"Arian is wrong, but he still can preach.

Before, he would not be beyond death's reach.

All property is secure to bring health.

That does not stop us from finding wealth."

GLADIUS SUPERBUS

"Return east where you will find no like kind.

Licinius long lost his life and mind.

His city thrives bearing Constantine's name.

The Edict will enjoy its own claim to fame."

Facing Pressure from the Huns, the Visi (Western Goths) Were Permitted to
Cross the Danube into the Empire to Live and Fight for Rome.
Now Facing Starvation, the Visi Revolt – 378 CE

CLAUDIUS

"Rome has its three islands and the Great Sea.

Two rivers buffer so all can be free

North Africa feeds the towns of the West.

Egypt fuels and sustains the rise of the rest."

FORTE

"Do you fear that we will now end our role?

Or, end up in ruins leaving some sole pole?

There are parts here you cannot now go.

Let alone the steppes where the winds do blow."

CLAUDIUS

"You are sage my friend as the steppes awake.

Scourge Huns move and made the Visi quake.

Gratian moves from Gaul to form a new host.

He wants to have the boar's baton the most."

FORTE

"Do we have a choice to obey this order?

How close we will reach the eastern border?

There are spirits there beyond our control.

There is more here than being on patrol."

CLAUDIUS

"You always have a choice to die instead.

But, your duty to Rome rests in your head.

Your honor and pride pulses in your heart.

When Caesar offered the chance then to start."

FORTE

"That was long ago and your mind is wrong.

My kin were sold then, but yes they were strong.

We serve, as we will, for God and our life.

How did the East come to such pain and strife?"

CLAUDIUS

"The Visi lept the Danube on the run.

They were pushed west by the savage Hun.

We broke a rule and gave them a new home.

They had to fight for us and cease to roam."

FORTE

"Why would guests start to attack and pillage?

Forcing me to leave my wife and village?

Some fight for Rome, but then turn on their host.

To defend their home and wife they love most."

CLAUDIUS

"They starved and Valens gave them no food.

He did not do what he promised he would.

They move to find a new home that they choose.

If they can do that, there is much to lose."

FORTE

"You cannot win a fight against this foe.

They are hungry and have no place to go.

They know your tactics, skill and no remorse.

They are much better with bows, spears and horse."

**The Adolescent Western Emperor Gratian Raises an Army in Northern Gaul
Led by the Frankish Chiefs Mallobaudes and Naniemus to Join His Uncle
the Eastern Emperor Valens to Fight the Visi**

EMPEROR GRATIAN

"We head east to join my uncle in war.

I will make good on the oath that I swore.

I have the best troops assembled in Gaul.

They have come so far to answer my call."

MALLOBAUDES

"You must stay or else your crown will be lost.

Going east now will be too much a cost.

Ninety days there and the same to get back.

They will forget you as soon as we attack."

NANIEMUS

"It is time for you to learn and not to fight.

We are old, but we are not afraid of the night.

We will bring glory to your name and house.

Your foes will tremble like a tiny mouse."

EMPEROR GRATIAN

"You both were younger in your first battle.

You did not have to hear such talk or prattle.

You fought and drew blood to make your name.

Now you lead my men because of your fame."

MALLOBAUDES

"We were not the emperor of the West.

Our elders told us what we must do best.

Read your Ambrose and Plato without fail.

We will return with a fateful tale."

Pascal Paul Piazza
**Mallobaudes and Naniemus and the Corsicans are Ambushed by King Priaus
and the Alemann Which are a German Tribe Which Ultimately
Do Not Survive Their Ambush**

NANIEMUS

"Ten days out and the spirit remains high.

These grizzled old souls do not fear to die.

They do this because they are good at it.

But, my friend, what bothers you as you sit."

MALLOBAUDES

"The Visi out east upset tribes out West.

The Allemann will find a way to test.

Crossing the Rhine while we are far away.

Trying to find gold and extend their sway."

KING PRIASUS

"Shout like a bear and feast on blood this day.

Woden has told us it is time to stay.

We take Gaul and kill their very young king.

Bells will chime our names when starting to ring."

NANIEMUS

"You old fool you are no match for us now.

You moan and move like a very old cow.

Did you think we only had one host?

Your head will still be ugly on a post."

KING PRIASUS

"Franks leading Romans you defile your kind.

Your flesh will rend being hard then to find.

My sword is longer than the axe you wield.

Blood from your heart will cover the whole field."

FORTE

"Not when you feel the cold tusk of this boar.

Driving straight and true through this older bore.

Let us kill their king and clear the whole field.

They will soon cry and die, run fast or yield."

MALLOBAUDES

"We have stern Corsicans and you do not.

Your head lay cut like a Gordian knot.

The vast field will suffer for ten more hours.

The blood will await the cleaning showers."

FORTE

"Many are dead, but many more retreat.

They will soon forget the sharp sting of defeat.

They must learn not to fight and to make peace.

So bloodbaths like this will very soon cease."

NANIEMUS

"You have learned well from too many wars.

We will follow and settle our old scores.

We will cross the Rhine and visit their home.

It is time they never again will roam."

FORTE

"They have dispersed and they cannot be found.

We searched up and down and all around.

It has been more than two months in and back.

Let us go East to join the attack."

Pascal Paul Piazza

**Sixtus Flumine and Aeneas, Survivors of the Devastating Loss at Adrianople,
Notify Mallobaudes and Naniemus and the Corsicans
of the Loss and the Death of the Eastern Emperor Valens by Fire**

MALLOBAUDES

"The Sun scorches this end of August day.

Twenty days has been the same in this way.

We cannot quick-march the men as it is hot.

Does old Valens still wait for us or not?"

NANIEMUS

"He dare not attack with just his own men.

He has been in town like cows in a pen.

He spent one year making peace with his foes.

The last four months will not induce any woes."

FORTE

"Two horsemen approach at a rapid pace.

The dust plumes framing great fear in their face.

Shields tight and form a full encircling square.

We will resolve this without any care."

SIXTUS FLUMINE

"Great Mars, we have found fresh Romans alive.

We come from where only a few survive.

Valens is dead being burned in the night.

There are but stacks of bodies from the fight."

AENEAS

"He was told that he would very well die.

The curse was strong for his Arian lie.

He could not stand that Gratian won his fight.

When he heard that he set out at first light."

SIXTUS FLUMINE

"Ten thousand was all he heard was in place.

It was time his men set out to race.

Eight hours in heat and fires aflame.

This is just one of the reasons to blame."

AENEAS

"He could not lose if he did not delay.

He was tired of what the mob would say.

But without your force he had a small host.

Tired and hot his men were tied to fear's post."

SIXTUS FLUMINE

"Then the horse descended crushing fast.

Skulls cracked and bodies did not last.

The hooves were like stars in a bleak dark night.

Leaving stacked corpses to seal the fight."

AENEAS

"They will not stay still or long where they are.

Their wood wagons are full and can move far.

Gratian is a foe that they still must fear.

They hope to draw you to them now from here."

MALLOBAUDES

"Then we will soon choose to the time and place.

We return home to a more guarded space.

We know their tactics better than they know.

They will not arrive before the first snow."

Pascal Paul Piazza

The Visi Settled Inside the Roman Empire.
After Five Years and No Attack, the Corsicans are Released from Service

F O R T E

"We train for years, but still await a battle.

Our only foes are some lost branded cattle.

They remind me of my home where I should be.

High in the maquis where honey is free."

N A N I E M U S

"I too would like to go back to my land.

But, it comes to me to hold in my hand.

Gratian told our Franks to join in his ranks.

He avoids war in favor of some thanks."

M A L L O B A U D E S

"Theodosius has settled the East.

The Visi and Goth farm there and soon feast.

New Rome and the Trinity are now one.

What once was slave now has fully won."

F O R T E

"As much as we would like to stay here in Gaul.

As far as we may roam we hear the call.

We belong on our island forever more.

We want now just to that warm rocky shore."

N A N I E M U S

"I wish you find peace and women to love.

And strength and honor from Woden above.

But, feuds and tribes cannot settle down long.

I will call the brave boar to fix more wrong."

**Forty-Six Years Later, the Visi Have Moved West, Sacked Rome,
and Are Rewarded Hegemony as Valuable Federates of Rome Over Southern Gaul
and Spain Including Corsica. The Visi Arrive at Aleria – 429 CE**

GROSSU

"Ten sails appear in control of our port.

One day we will have to build us a fort.

We have seen this so many times before.

Just another chapter in our changing lore."

CERTU

"The new Roman tribune arrives today.

That does not seem to disrupt anyone's day.

There has not been a tribune for so long.

It was like we no longer seemed to belong."

EBER

"Get me quick off this wretched wooden ship.

I do not care if I fall or if I slip.

Give me a wagon with four wheels so round.

Give me solid, firm and not moving ground."

BÄR

"You bow to your people on hands and knees.

You honor the stones as much as the trees.

They laugh too much to give us our just due.

The dock is wet just like a new morning dew."

GROSSU

"Did you want us to erect you an arch?

So you could crawl as your army did march?

Must we tremble in fear to Rome's new might?

You should leave right now before it is night."

CERTU

"My eyes see Rome, but no Romans are here!

My eyes lie like I drank too much fresh beer.

They are too tall with hair so straight and brown.

The lack humor and hide behind a frown."

EBER

"We are the Visi and Rome sent us here.

Corsica is now within our large sphere.

Aetius set us up in southern Gaul.

We rule there, here and most of Spain not all."

BÄR

"We are not here to collect any tax.

We want trade in resin, honey and wax.

We do not want slaves, as all men are free.

We want to find wealth on land not the sea."

GROSSU

"Did you not sack Rome with steel and fire?

The world's mother cried beside a pyre.

You broke her back opening the shut door.

And, there came Vandals, Alans and much more?"

CERTU

"We heard that you burn men alive and cheer.

That you are cruel and live off other's fear.

Rome made you her guest when you needed help.

You then chortled when you made Valens yelp."

EBER

"We have heard that this is savage place.

That you are a lying disgraceful race.

We cannot rely on what we are told.

We must let the facts themselves now unfold."

BÄR

"Rome was a shell, but a point could be made.

We did not put any church to flame or blade.

Alaric had to show that he had worth.

That he could sack the mother of the earth."

GROSSU

"Do you have such a point to make to us?

That we should bow, scape and make a great fuss?

Your three hundred men may build a small fort.

But legions have been lost leaving this port."

CERTU

"Rome holds the coast but the villages are free.

You will find no ripe tree or honey bee.

They will defend their homes like a mad boar.

Rome knew to stay here and stop any war."

EBER

"We will defend your home to our last spear.

That is why we have three-hundred men here.

What we did before was to find a home.

Now, we have one and we will never roam."

BÄR

"Our oath to be Rome is so strong and pure.

Our faith in our duty will long endure.

We will camp outside so we do not mix.

There should be few problems we have to fix."

GROSSU

"To Rome, did you not swear an oath to her?

But, you betrayed her like a rabid cur!

We live to be true to our solemn bond.

Not to change course in the first shallow pond."

CERTU

"Twice, you came to Gaul and lost on the field.

Yet, you came back to Rome and did not yield.

You took over lands which were long settled.

You are now where you should not have mettled."

EBER

"The few that run Rome put us in our place.

We did not displace the Gaul from his space.

Rather, Gaul was Rome from an early date.

We will now be Rome on a new blank slate."

BÄR

"We will run affairs with a simple plan.

We will use Latin as much as we can.

There is a threat that should concern us more.

The Vandals have the North African shore."

CHAPTER FIFTEEN

The Roman Quintet – The Further Transformation of
The Mantle or Rome 440CE – 470CE

HYPERBOLEUM

"Some pagans remain as the face of Rome.

Making martyrs on the path that they roam.

The new Rome transforms her of her pagan past.

The process is slow and not very fast."

DELERIUM

"The Visi rule with a firm even hand.

They secure most of Gaul and Spain's main land.

They are the face of Rome's laws and orders.

But, armies still try to re-write her borders."

PESSIMISSIUM

"Vandals occupy the West's source of food.

Inheriting a grand navy of wood.

The Huns invade Gaul to consume the West.

Putting the new Rome to a stringent test."

MARY

"The West is saved for at least fifteen years.

The Visi and generals crush all fears.

The Huns withdraw with no claims to the crown.

Vandal ambition is often put down."

CHARLOTTE

"The Vandals sack Rome as her newest face.

They invade Corsica at a fast pace.

'Til five years of attrition makes its mark.

The lack of full control remains quite stark."

Pascal Paul Piazza
The Visi Leaders Eber and Bär and the Corsicans Grossu and Certu Are Concerned About a Remaining Pagan Roman Leader in the Capu Corsu Persecuting Christians Like the Vandal Gaiseric – 440 CE

GROSSU

"Eber did not lie about Visi rule.

It ignored each mountain village and mule.

They kept apart honoring our joint law.

Good faith fully reigned from what we all saw."

CERTU

"Bär was so right about the Vandals' action.

They easily beat the main Roman faction.

They have Carthage now with its ships to sail.

They soon cut off the West's wheat as blackmail."

EBER

"Gaiseric wants to show that he is strong.

He persecutes Christians he thinks are wrong.

Not because of doctrine but for power.

He alone seeks to top the tallest tower."

BÄR

"A pagan prefect rules on the wrong course.

Who acts with caprice and with no remorse.

An heir to prefects over many years.

He hates all Christians and fulminates fears."

WACHSAN

"I will go north to Bastia today.

The edicts permit Christians to pray.

Tenure does not excuse breach of the law.

I will silence this false crow and his caw."

**The Pagan Prefect Flexi Saxo Hosts a Bacchanalia in the Capu Corsu and Requires
the Visiting Eusebius of Carthage to Make St. Julia, His Slave, Honor the Roman Gods
Which She Refuses to Do and is Killed**

PREFECT FELIX SAXO

"We slice the bull's neck to give us new life.

The vigor of the blood destroys all strife.

We drink 'til Bacchus finds comfort and rest.

We find peace in a woman's naked breast."

EUSEBIUS

"I come from Carthage with its Vandal king.

I am a merchant with such gifts to bring.

I have pearls to place 'round her nubile neck.

Taken now from a sunken Punic wreck."

PREFECT FELIX SAXO

"But, you hide a pure prize among the best.

One that is more valuable than the rest.

Bring her quickly from your ship tonight.

We pause to welcome such a new delight."

EUSEBIUS

"She is my mirror of how I should act.

She acts for virtue and with timeless tact.

She serves without fear and with selfless grace.

My respect secures her far from this place."

PREFECT FELIX SAXO

"How dare you reject my power and might.

She will honor our gods within our sight.

She is a slave with no master to lead.

I will pay you whatever price you need."

EUSEBIUS

"I cannot convince her to change her mind.
I would flog her, but she is warm and kind.
There is no one else like her that I know.
She is the Sun that shines and winds that blow."

FELIX SAXO

"I have gold to give and vast land to deed.
Four handmaids would be yours for any need.
But, you are worthless and I tire fast.
Girl, I grant you your freedom at long last."

JULIA

"I am now as free as I want to be.
I honor my Lord and have his words to see.
I will not praise your gods on any day.
In fact, I defile them in my own way."

FELIX SAXO

"Then flog her twice and tie her to a cross.
One less smug Christian is not a great loss.
You may fast, yet your red blood will still flow.
You can wretch in your position so low."

JULIA

"You honor Him who was beaten with whips.
I will die as He did with blood pierced hips.
I now pass in joy saved by His love.
I truly am free transformed into a dove."

**Wachshan, the Visi Leader, Arrives After St. Julia is Martyred to Enforce
the Still Valid Edict of Toleration Which Guaranteed St. Julia
The Right to Worship as She Wanted to Do**

LEGIONNAIRE

"Take her bones as holy relics to hold.

This is a true story long to be told.

All of our troops must retreat from this place.

The prefect broods in despair and disgrace."

WACHSAN

"My men just arrived and we need to eat.

What happened here that we need to retreat?

We have come to enforce the edicts true.

The glory that is Rome extends here too."

FELIX SAXO

"He saw a magic show and nothing more.

She became a dove and flew out the door.

I beat the Christian and she took her licks

She left with smoke and many other tricks."

WACHSAN

"All have the right to worship as they wish.

Not to be beaten or cut like a fish.

Rome is Christian if you like it or not.

The edicts are true and they were not bought."

FELIX SAXO

"Then my Rome has long died if you are right.

There is no need to continue to fight.

My gladius was the symbol of might.

I stab myself with pride in your lone sight."

Pascal Paul Piazza

The Roman Generals Stilicho, Aetius, Ricimer and Avitus Were the True Power Brokers.
Avitus, son of a Roman Senator in Gaul. Entreats the Visi Theodoric
to Join the Fight Against Attila the Hun – 451 CE

AVITUS

"The Huns invade Gaul and threaten your home.

They were why you long ago entered Rome.

They are the scourge of God and all things good.

Aetius does not have the troops he should."

THEODORIC

"You fear you will lose your Senator's house.

You try to flush us out like an old grouse.

You want us to fight with many to die.

You will invoke our faith with some new lie."

AVITUS

"The blood flows fast from the Marne to the Seine.

Arrows blacken the sky and fall like rain.

The girl who saved Paris is not here.

Burnt flesh and cries coalesce in fear."

THEODORIC

"Aetius and you chart where we must be.

Alans there and we here next to the Sea.

We sent away all the Vandals for you.

Yet, they have Carthage starving the West too."

AVITUS

"You are Rome and the heir to her great name.

Her heroes wanted to add to her fame.

Bring troops you have from within your wide sphere.

Your faith and mission are now set and clear."

WACHSAN

"The Huns form a mass at the city gate.

We must attack before it is too late.

At this point, they must all fight without horse.

Losing their skill as a matter of course."

EHRE

"The Alans feigned that they would not fight.

Luring the Huns to move within sight.

Let us spite the Huns for their vicious past.

My Corsicans ram them with a boar's blast."

ISSU

"Raise the baton standard for all to see.

We fight to keep our own families free.

Our shields are smaller than they use to be.

But still cover spears that sting like a bee."

FORSI

"Three hundred in tight formation is strong.

Our steel will point out how they are so wrong.

The weight of our core mass will break their line.

Double time march will soon win us some wine."

WACHSAN

"We fought for five hours 'til the Sun did set.

They left still ready to do battle yet.

They sought plains where they fight at their best.

With bodies piled high from this long test."

SANGIBAN

"We are now secure behind our main gate.

They regroup for the fight fostered by fate.

Things would be lost with Huns inside the wall.

From such a base all of Gaul would soon fall."

ISSU

"We heard tales of their skill with bow and horse.

They will kill to laugh and have no remorse.

By why do Gepids and Goths stay so near?

When we are told to deal with them in fear?"

WACHSAN

"Attila is a clever, simple man.

He weds to ally with all tribes he can.

He uses a wooden cup but gives out gold.

He will slice your heart with a blade so cold."

FORSI

"So, there is no honor in how they fight.

It is gold that gilds their courage and might.

Their sure skill makes them a force to be seen.

They lack faith just as they are cold and mean."

EHRE

"When we act we seek to build our own home.

The Huns care less and simply like to roam.

Rome is an idea built by flawed men.

They hate that idea so we now must win."

The Roman-Visi-Alan-Corsican Order at the Battle of Chalons sur Marne

AETIUS

"The Hun has chosen his battlefield well.

A long flat plain sloping up to a dell.

The fear of our horse will narrow the field.

The mass of our troops will cause them to yield."

SANGIBAN

"We will form the center and hold your right.

The rain of our arrows will start the fight.

We Alans have a debt to claim from before.

They will not know what we will have in store."

THEODORIC

"I command the day with my Visi host.

We will accept and reject foes the most.

I will ride tall daring for all to see.

My men will be a wall in front of me."

THORISMUND

"My Visi horse will charge from the far right.

We will be hidden from Attila's sight.

The certain ground favors our heavy horse.

This is not the steppes where they rule the course."

ISSU

"We will be the pivot for horse and host.

Troops there and then not like a magic ghost.

The baton is forthright, fair and ever strong.

We are Rome today and cannot be wrong."

Pascal Paul Piazza

The Hunnic-Ostrogoth-Gepid Order at the Battle of Chalons sur Marne

ATTILA

"I like what my seers divine this day.

A leader will die in a wretched way.

Aetius has enjoyed his fervent life.

His death will seed both discord and such strife."

ARDARIC

"Let the Gepids attack the Roman line.

It is thin, weak and young twisting like twine.

They will not see your strike just like lighting.

It will create conditions so frightening."

ATTILA

"You will get your chance, but just not right now.

The Romans defend like a vestige cow.

The center will fall with the left and right.

This battle will end with very little fight."

ARDARIC

"You want Goths and Germans to fight their own.

Not those for whom our hatred has been sown.

It is like we are looking at our kin.

It may be hard even to order our men."

ATTILA

"Are these soldiers or cowards on the field?

It is time to grab your sword and your shield.

Attacks the Alans forcing a retreat.

Smite the Visi and Rome will be beat."

The Battle of Chalons sur Marne and Aftermath

FORSI

"War is never like the tales that are told.

The blood and gore make none of us bold.

Horse and troops hit the Alans with one punch.

We fought hand-to-hand in a confused bunch."

WACHSAN

"The Hunnish horse did not impact its blow.

The Alans shook some but were not laid low.

They held 'tho seven of ten would soon die.

Pools of blood made rest for bodies to lie."

EHRE

"This was not a fight for arrow or bow.

This was sword-to-sword in row after row.

The Visi horse then struck with its firm might.

Breaking the Huns' back in this earnest fight."

ISSU

"The Romans next hit the Gepids with force.

The Gepids fought but lost in a short course.

The Visi then forced the retreat of its foes.

But, its king was shot turning joy to woes."

FORSI

"Thorismund stepped up and kept the order.

The Huns and Goths were sent to their border.

We then planted the baton of the boar.

This was the sharp end of this gruesome war."

THORISMUND

"We should chase them and destroy them for good.

That is why you made us Rome when you could.

We must purge the scourge of God and of man.

When we have the chance to do so and can."

AETIUS

"I mourn your father and the loss of men.

 You are young and your blood boils for your vim.

You must return home as you are the king.

In your absence, others will claim the ring."

WACHSAN

"You are clever, but here your words seem true.

What your real motive is I have no clue.

Yet, we did not win here to lose our home.

Or, to shake free from the mantle of Rome."

EHRE

"Wachsan and I can stay with our old friends.

These Corsicans will help make amends.

There were Franks on both sides of today's fight.

It is time for the night to feed the light."

ISSU

"We still have two hundred for a camp.

It is night so let us light an oil lamp.

We will mark this day with a brand new town.

And defeat those who try to tear it down."

The Corsican Diaspora Begins Because of a Beautiful Strong Woman Basina Who Acts to Protect the Land When the Frankish Leader Clothar Will Not

FORSI

"We have found some land that is dry not damp.

Near to the Marne where we will make our camp.

Our camp will be the outline for a town.

We will now newly build and not tear down."

ISSU

"There is a tall woman with a long staff.

Asking where will she split the wheat from chaff.

She shouts that we have stolen her mill site.

As the magnate can you muzzle her bite?"

CLOTHAR

"I have no power over her when she acts.

She states Salic Law the best with facts.

She has always had longer hair than me.

She tonsors me with her wit being free."

FORSI

"She is like a Corsican woman fair.

They will carve you up without any care.

But, they respond to the fair, forthright man.

And then give more than they will know or can."

ISSU

"I know you can fight a vile Goth or Hun.

You are no match for her under the Sun.

If you must, let us now go save the men.

I will laugh to see you cut like a hen!"

BASINA

"Do you think you can simply steal our land?

Which we own and work with our own hand.

This is my grist mill which I use for oats.

Not some pasture for pleasure or for goats."

FORSI

"Clothar the magnate gave us a new deed.

To build a new town for all that you need.

There will springs, mills, forums and bath.

New roads and forum will chart a new path."

BASINA

"He cannot give you what he does not own.

He is a chief, but we own what is sown.

There are no Roman taxes that we pay.

We decide when and how we spend each day."

FORSI

"You are free because we spilled our blood.

A sanguine path poured forth like a flood.

To cover the ground so you still may seed.

And grow the good grain upon which to feed."

BASINA

"We thank you for the sacrifice you made.

We can make a deal by hand not a blade.

The town will be for all of us to use.

With a marketplace where no one will lose."

ISSU

"I did not think we would last a full year.

The completion of the town is so near.

We live on our own, but the Franks are friends.

From the fateful start, we have made amends."

FORSI

"She is why we live in a constant peace.

We are here to serve not search for some fleece.

They make too much money selling us food.

But, the men are happy and that is good."

BASINA

"You are truly like the stories we heard.

Your totem stood with us above the herd.

You act like this always has been your home.

Knowing that you are here to rule as Rome."

ISSU

"We are our village from where we were born.

It is our fabric which cannot be torn.

Life's sure struggle makes equals of us all.

It is hard to stand and easy to fall."

FORSI

"I have relatives just as I find here.

You could be my cousin or sister dear.

The same sounds tack the Sun in its own race.

The center of it all is this one place."

CLOTHAR

"It has been five years and your job is done.

Attila died and the Hun war is won.

Basina comes to thank you for all.

I have never seen a woman so tall."

BASINA

"Do I have to kiss you to show desire?

Does not a gold chord necklace start a fire?

You are set to leave with no kiss to show.

Do I cause you pain and suffering so?"

FORSI

"You are the whole Sun and Moon to me now.

I sought to say, but I did not know how.

Plus, you have a father and brother too.

I insult them to show my love for you."

BASINA

"By Woden, when will you men start to know.

You have to plant a seed for a plant to grow.

I hope our children learn faster than you.

You really did not have much of a clue."

ISSU

"The rest of us long for the Sea and home.

We have served our faith, honor and Rome.

We join Ricimer on his march from here.

Best health as you both have nothing to fear."

Ricimer Defeats the Vandals Off Corsica – 456 CE

ISSU

"We have been on the road for many weeks.

The coast invites me beyond all the peaks.

Why are there forty ships waiting to sail?

Is there news of my home you need to tell?"

RICIMER

"My status grows hosting such fabled troops.

The Visi cannot rule jumping through hoops.

They will chase Sueves in Spain for the next years.

I will fill this void and allay all fears."

FLAVIUS GRACCHUS

"Our spies tell us that the Vandals move north.

Intent to put Aleria to the torch.

While we are here Rome will protect its wealth.

Corsica feeds us and promotes our health."

TIBERIAS OF HIPPO

"Aetius sent the Vandals from the West.

To struggle for power at Hippo at best.

But they beat all 'til Carthage was lost.

The loss of North Africa was quite a cost."

RICIMER

"Gaiseric found ships ready for his war.

He attacks east and then west seeking more.

He wants your home for its resin and wood.

More ships isolate the West more if he could."

ISSU

"We go to where Dido lost in her quest.

The ships from Carthage failed in that test.

One thousand years ago repeat today.

My home again will survive on this day."

FLAVIUS GRACCHUS

"The black sails appear on the starboard side.

Greeks sail their ships for money and not pride.

Ten rows of five ships lure us to attack.

Instead, we will soon maneuver and tack."

TIBERIAS OF HIPPO

"They want us to get so close we cannot move.

To line us up like we were in a groove.

We will keep our strength and distance apart.

We will decide when this battle will start."

RICIMER

"These Goths are not sailors and cannot wait.

Our delay frustrates them and tempts their fate.

They break their lines exposing each ship.

We pounce watching wood burn and each sail rip."

ISSU

"I had never seen such a one-sided win.

I would have such tales to tell all my kin.

We are going home now after this fight.

The water is clear in the Moon's bright light."

Gaiseric Did Not Stop After the Defeat By Ricimer. Gaiseric Wants to Be Like Stilicho, Aetius, Ricimer and Avitus. He, Huneric and the Vandals Invade Corsica Again – 465 CE

GAISERIC

"I remember the defeat nine years hence.

Facts on the ground have changed a lot since.

The East has given me a lasting peace.

Fights among Rome's general do not cease."

HUNERIC

"There is no one to stop us from our task.

Rome hides in Milan under a false mask.

The West is alone when Corsica falls.

The emperor will quake behind his walls."

GAISERIC

"I sacked Rome to stake my own clear claim.

I burnt no churches and hurt just the lame.

I have power to do what I choose.

Ricimer and Avitus will soon lose."

HUNERIC

"Corsica has wood, fine resin and wax.

We want their resources and not their tax.

We can build the largest navy around.

We no longer have to fight on ground."

GAISERIC

"The Huns chased us into Rome's embrace.

They are now dispersed all over the place.

The Visi pushed us into this great boat.

When we strangle trade we will surely gloat."

ISSU

"Black sails fully fill Aleria's port.

We have seen before action of this sort.

But, I have seen the Vandals fight at sea.

This is not the same as it seems to be."

WACHSAN

"This standard and I are all that is Rome.

Euric and his brother fight now at home.

All troops did return to join either side.

There will be three of us and our own pride."

PRATU

"All have withdrawn to a mountain village.

The Vandals come and they may pillage.

But, they will find no food, slaves or gold.

Even when they march to the rocks so cold."

ISSU

"Each of our villages will be secluded deep.

We will then be able to keep the peace.

'Til they try to attack on narrow paths.

Then rock and rivers will become blood baths."

WACHSAN

"We should have one leader to meet their king.

We should not bow, kneel or kiss his fine ring.

Issu's plan has given us lasting hope.

We can win in the end this and not just cope."

GAISERIC

"Where is the fanfare and nymphs from the Sea.

I am heir to Scipio and Pompey.

Avitus and Ricimer fear my name.

Rome should hasten to embrace my fast fame."

ISSU

"A silent wind plays flute and waves are cymbals.

The empty roads care not for your symbols.

There is plenty of resin, wax and wood.

Yet, you conquer no one even if you could."

GAISERIC

"I sacked Rome ten years ago because I could.

It burned just in parts as I said it would.

I am the same as those here before me.

This will be a new Rome for all to see."

ISSU

"You can live in the Visi camp if you choose.

Build great ships you think cannot ever lose.

Attack us and ten thousand troops will die.

You will never hold our own mountains high."

GAISERIC

"Burn the whole town down to the mottled sand.

We will build our camp on our chosen land.

Let these three go and watch were they will go.

We will awaken them with horse and bow."

GELIMER

"We are four days by our base camp by day.
We left the wagons fourteen miles away.
Ten women slit the throats of our rear guard.
Burnt wagon parts were strewn across the yard."

HILDERIC

"One thousand fearful men march in single file.
Stretched and open along the course of a mile.
Double time with shields high above your heads.
Soon we will find some ground for your lost beds."

GELIMER

"What sound echoes loud as the blue schist shakes?
I fear hooves and snorts as our line now breaks.
Bulls rage in front and boars press in the rear.
Arrows kill those not trampled with fear."

HILDERIC

"Three hundred retreat at a jumbled pace.
Enter the woods to find a refuge space,
Restore ranks and enter the woods as one.
Do not do what the first hundred have done."

GELIMER

"We return with only fifty odd men.
These paths are designed as a killing pin.
We continue to build ships that we need.
But, we will not have any troops to lead."

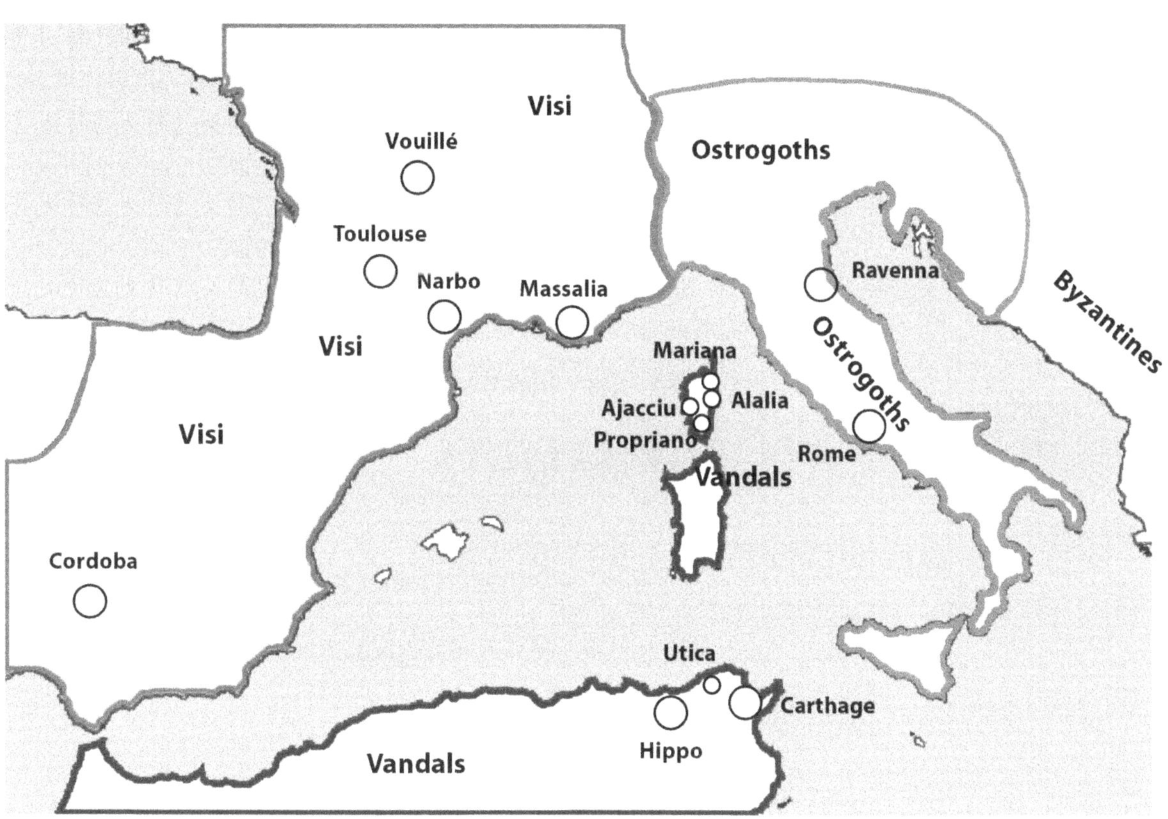

Visa Kingdom - 500 CE

Peace at the Vandal Camp (Regnum Vandalorum) - 470 CE

GAISERIC

"We have created a culture on the coast.

Latin and law of a new Rome to boast.

Yet, I have lost ten thousand men to date.

Your threat has been made whole as our true fate."

ISSU

"Your hubris blinds you from that in plain sight.

You will never find us despite your might.

We like our home even if you do not.

We are bound tight like a Gordian knot."

GAISERIC

"You mean I choke and have no blade to cut.

I am a mouflon that just needs to rut.

How can Rome rule you but we cannot too?

What truce can there be that will honor me?"

ISSU

"Honor is earned and not a free gift.

After five years let us now close the rift.

Take no slaves and let us rest in peace more.

You can say that you alone won the war."

GAISERIC

"You deserve such terms to tell many tales.

We work as one to make short ships and sails.

We are more Roman than the Visi are.

Let us dress our wounds and cover each scar."

CHAPTER SIXTEEN

Pascal Paul Piazza

The Succession: Vandals to Byzantines to Goths to Byzantines
470 CE – 710 CE

HYPERBOLIUM

"The mantle of Rome rests with certain kings.

Latin in name, text, law, money and things.

Rome was Toulouse, Carthage and Ravenna.

Goths are now first counsels just like Cinna."

DELIRIUM

"Goths sack Rome 'til Goths sack Goths in a row.

Some Goths bow East to keep the West in tow.

Each king was allowed to rule his own state.

Each king may expand securing his own fate."

PESSIMISSIUM

"Corsicans bristled under Vandal rule.

They felt no better off than an old mule.

Some preferred diaspora to return.

One saw the Saxon wagons and tents burn."

MARY

"Some with the Franks saw the Visi state shrink.

The Franks were there to help those on the brink.

The East sought to restore Rome to its pride.

'Til taxes yoked more flesh from the hide."

CHARLOTTE

"The maquis withdrew to its daily life.

That provided them enough pain and strife.

Corsica now on was ruled from afar.

No need to question who the rulers are."

Ursu's Quest: 495 CE

FORSI

"Son, I can see my village in my head.

I will always be home 'til I am dead.

We are with the Franks, but I am still home.

No matter how far from there I may roam."

BASINA

"You have become thirty years old this day.

You have so excelled in the Frankish way.

But, you are not whole and lack a full heart.

Your quest for your own village now must start."

URSU

"I have heard all of the stories you tell.

My name recalls deeds of how to act well.

I seek out our village which invites me.

I will be fully forthright, fair and free."

FORSI

"You must complete this journey on your own.

The seeds of your true path have long been sown.

Words will not help you finish the long path.

Wits and lessons will overcome all wrath."

BASINA

"Go southwest and south to the Visi hall.

Eber will not believe you are so tall.

You will travel near to the Breton land.

Then to where Cor began his trip so grand."

Near the Breton Border

A TALKING MOUFLON

"That is a solid chestnut walking staff.

It should certainly deter the riff-raff.

I have not seen one like it around here.

Many will covet to own it I fear."

URSU

"It is one way my family will know me.

Carved from trees that I so long to see.

But, it is yours if you are in such need.

Although I am not sure what is your breed?"

A TALKING MOUFLON

"Does not a talking ram bother you so?

If not, I come from where you want to go.

I know a path to a village on high.

To find what you now seek and touch the sky."

URSU

"How can you know the secret of my quest?

What casts the journey that for me is best?

Do you deceive me to stray from my path?

And suffer a lifetime of endless wrath?"

A TALKING MOUFLON

"This is the crossroad you were meant to find.

You were taught to pass a test of this kind.

Go to the endless forest without haste.

Then to Carhaix while you are still chaste."

Ursu Contemplates Entering Brittany

URSU

"My reflection was right before my face.

Did I miss it as I was out of place?

Do I have a truthful path to follow?

Or, was I waylaid by wry words so hollow?"

CLOVIS

"I would welcome a sign to guide my way.

The edge of my ax dictates my whole day.

The forest calls you so do not delay.

You are extremely lucky I would say."

URSU

"I go where I have never been before.

I do not know what disputes are in store.

I must refresh my water and find food.

Do you know some nearby place where I could?"

CLOVIS

"Do you hear the crystalline voice that sings?

You have been called by the hidden spring.

It welcomes you to refresh and drink your fill.

And be master of every tree and hill."

URSU

"I have much to drink for over one week.

I will find the meat and grains that I seek.

You have led and provided great relief.

Soon, my young Frank, they will call you chief."

Pascal Paul Piazza

In the Broceliande Forest or the Mythical Forest of No Return

U R S U

"I am three days in the forest by foot.

Charcoal leaves swirl covering my staff with soot.

I pass a burnt field with men now in sight.

So, I ask where I may soon stay the night."

B E D I V E R E

"There are rooms for you in the great estate.

You will feel like you were sent here by fate.

Its name has always been Val sans Retour.

Its drink and food provide the perfect cure."

U R S U

"I need bedding tonight to rest my head.

When I sleep you will think that I am dead.

But, your faces should be flush with fresh life.

Yet, I surmise a senseless strident strife."

B O R S

"We have no wants, will or group desires.

All fear, grief, hope and laughter expires.

We have a perfect life for us indeed

We receive all that it is that we need."

U R S U

"This must be why I had to come here.

The answers to my questions seem clear.

I will seek quarters for the night and day.

I thank you both for what you had to say."

In the Estate of Circe

CIRCE

"Welcome, I am Circe and this is my home.

You will love it here and not want to roam.

I provide each want and pleasure to see.

So, fall down to your knees and embrace me."

URSU

"I kneel to no one as I was born free.

I act for my own tribe and not for me.

I travel a road that looks to be best.

I came for a place and a bed to rest."

CIRCE

"You are a warrior looking for the Grail

It lay in a room where time does not tell.

You quest to know now what you cannot lose.

Drink from the answers in the cup you choose."

URSU

"These are not verses in some hoary tale.

There are no high heroic deeds to tell.

I am common and I travel this night.

Waiting for the dawn of a morn so bright."

CIRCE

"I can be any woman you desire.

Glistening skin lures the lust you aspire.

 No, there is a special room just for you.

I have waited long years to test her too."

Pascal Paul Piazza

The Chambers of Guinevere

U R S U

"I wonder why she chose this certain room.

A round table, open Ambrose and a broom.

A couch ready for me to rest my head.

And, Freyja made flesh sitting on a bed."

G U I N E V E R E

"I do not recall inviting a guest.

Did you come to talk about some quest?

Or, discuss some theology this night?

Does my breast shine in the gossamer light?"

U R S U

"I will avert my eyes and leave right now.

I ask forgiveness as I take a bow.

Circe told me that I could find

rest here. This has been such a huge mistake I fear."

G U I N E V E R E

"Do not leave as I was just having fun.

Come find constant joy like a youthful pun.

My setter Max protects me from distress.

Sleep on the couch for relief from all stress."

U R S U

"Thank you for your kindness and open heart.

We should talk some before my sleep starts.

Please tell me about your life in this place.

Why you smile and have no lines on your face."

GUINEVERE

"Max and I came when he was just a pup.
My hair was short when I drank from the cup.
We have been here maybe forty days long.
The whole time happy and singing a song."

URSU

"I fear and do not want you to despair.
Your feet and gown hide the length of your hair.
Max is old searching for his final bog.
The men I met and you are in a fog."

GUINEVERE

"We are in a mass miasma of joy.
We do what we want as time remains coy.
Drink and eat what Circe provides for us.
You will find solace and not make a fuss."

URSU

"Remember your Homeric text and verse.
Thus, I did not drink and have been so terse.
You are slaves to what you eat and drink.
Taste this spring water that will help you think."

GUINEVERE

"The water has helped me to be reborn.
Mending the curtain of life that is torn.
Lancelot sought to rescue me from here.
But, I would not ever let him come near."

URSU

"We must let all your men have a full taste.

Revive them to rise above all this waste.

But, we must pretend to do as she wants.

'Til all can drink fully from the spring fonts."

GUINEVERE

"I will send Bedivere to tap the spring.

Bors will bring Lancelot my golden ring.

He will bring an army to siege this place.

'Til then, let Circe see you with my lace."

CIRCE

"I do not trust this new ram with the sheep.

His true core will disturb their sudden sleep.

Have your troops ready to defend my grounds.

My gratitude will be great without bounds."

KING CLAUDUS

"To serve you is all the reward we seek.

With more meat and mead our morale will peak.

Your guests will not know how and why we act.

Just to be here creates such a joyous fact."

CIRCE

"You have served me well for some twenty years.

Since you sent Guinevere here for her fears.

I have a task that only I can do.

There is an old friendship I must renew."

In the Cave Des Faux Amants (Cave of False Love)

D E B

"Merlin, was lust worth your current disgrace?

You look so old in your white hair and face.

Frozen in ice and time with your magic.

What you taught her is something so tragic."

M E R L I N

"Yet, you revive me when you have a chance.

Freeing me to soar from that tragic trance.

I was truly in love with one so dear.

Who then imprisoned me for good in here."

V I V I A N E

"Deb confounds love as the true twin of lust.

She has not known a love she could trust.

I will freeze you two together for life.

 And return as Circe to support strife."

D E B

"Merlin was blinded to your true deceit.

He gave you his soul as a selfless feat.

He gave you power over his own heart.

But none over the conflict about to start."

M E R L I N

"I am the fire that made the shapeless land.

Not the flame from my heart to your cold hand.

Draw forth all blood and water from your bone.

You are now another cold standing stone."

D E B

"Take her to stand in the field at Carnac.

Let us watch as they prepare an attack.

The defense will break when her death is known.

A kingdom arises when hope is sown."

M E R L I N

"Lancelot will lead and dictate the fight.

Gawain will charge with horse from the right

Ossetian will support with skilled bow.

Galahad will face the retreating foe."

D E B

"Our forces move deftly with such great skill.

The defense moves with fear and lack of will.

The bloodshed will force them quickly to yield.

We secure the advantage on this field."

M E R L I N

"Arthur sent brave men to rescue a queen.

Circe was stronger than it was foreseen.

I do not know this last man to arrive.

His valor allowed us all to survive."

D E B

"He is Ursu half Corsican and Frank.

He cares little for power or high rank.

I sent him here to meet your mind's request.

Let them go from Carhaix on his own quest."

***Guinevere, Lancelot, Gawain, Tristan, Bedivere, Bors and Ursu Travel To Cornwall
(Which is Directly Across from Brittany) to Tintagel and to
Meet King Leodegrance (Guinevere's Father)***

LANCELOT

"We track the route done by many before.

I ride ahead to see what is instore.

Raise the ram banner of Carhaix up high.

Let the sign of her return light the sky."

GUINEVERE

"He sees me but he does not look at all.

To him I must be covered in a pall.

Did you not lust when you saw me at first?

Was I the potion that quenched love's thirst?"

URSU

"It does not matter what I thought of you.

That I was impressed at once is quite true.

I would not touch you even if I dare.

I would not so dishonor one so fair."

KING LEODEGRANCE

"Daughter my heart races to see your face.

But, Arthur is in need of men and grace.

He stands alone with his sword in his hand.

Facing Saxons devouring the land."

TRISTAN

"Arthur sent me with details of a plan.

To find the soul of Britain if I can.

To rescue Guinevere who is the land.

And to find comrades waiting for command."

Arthur, Guinevere, Lancelot, Gawain, Tristan, Bedivere, Bors and Ursu Address the Unwelcome Saxon Army at the Battle of Mount Badon – 495 CE

ARTHUR

"I hold Rome's standard standing true and tall.

It commands the field like Hadrian's Wall.

No Saxon will pass except on his shield.

It is time to go home or hereby yield."

GUINEVERE

"Britain stands too in all of her vast might.

Her many tribes expand before your sight.

Many arrows will fly like geese in flight.

There is no way that we will lose this fight."

URSU

"My chestnut staff will stave off your attack.

Bedivere, Bors and I will drive you back.

Arthur and I are both named for the bear.

You know that you do not attack a lair."

OSSETIAN

"We are steppe horse archers with compound bows.

They make easy targets in your straight rows.

We are also skilled in use of the lance.

We move so fast as if you were in a trance."

LANCELOT

"If you have honor send out your best man.

He and I will fight to the death as we can.

We may save the lives of many today.

And not lose arms and legs in a cruel way."

Deb and Merlin Discuss Their Decreasing Role and the Results of the Battle of Mount Badon

MERLIN

"We should not intervene despite the odds.

They no longer need us or standing stone gods.

This is the time for humanity's deeds.

Their new God now meets all of their needs."

DEB

"Yet, I relish the chance to be there some day.

To supply guidance with words I may say.

We saw the best and the worst they can be.

Some day we may cover them with the Sea."

MERLIN

"Arthur's troops moved avoiding static lines.

Gawain cut the Saxon front like weak vines.

Ursu was the pivot for the main moves.

The Saxons fell under the galloping hooves."

DEB

"The arrow flurry turned the day into night.

Leaving piles of dead bodies in the fight.

Arthur and Lancelot killed the Saxon kings.

The Saxons left dropping most of their things."

MERLIN

"The standards were high and the bells did ring.

Telling the brave deeds of footmen and king.

The Saxons would soon leave for several years.

Optimism would replace the high fears."

Arthur and Guinevere Become the King and Queen At Tintagel in Cornwall Inviting the Valiant Soldiers to Stay Around a Round Table and Preserve the Land

ARTHUR

"We mourn our dead and give thanks for our win.

On this bold field we each confess our sin.

For unity, Guinevere and I will wed.

And produce the next heir from our true bed."

KING LEODEGRANCE

"We do not need an old king who cannot fight.

I resign in Arthur's favor this night.

I endow a gift as I am still able.

I give you a universal round table."

GUINEVERE

"There will be a seat for the fourteen who fought.

That is but one seat that cannot be bought.

Arthur and I will sit as east and west.

This table will seat only the very best."

LANCELOT

"I cannot stay as plots are being made.

I best can decide things with my bold blade.

I have a seat to come to when you call.

I give blessings and well wishes to all."

URSU

"I should leave too as my trip just began.

I should depart tomorrow when I can.

It is the hardest decision to make.

The bonds I found here may not even break."

After Twelve Years Helping the Round Table Soldiers Ursu Returns to the Spring Outside Brittany to Meet King Clovis of the Franks Who Has Defeated the Visi and Others and Expanded His Domain – 507 CE

URSU

"It looks the same even after twelve years.

Its waters have known joy and mournful tears.

Its sweet taste is as I remember before.

As I embark to the Corsican shore."

CLOTHAR

"How dare you drink from King Clovis' own well?

You act like it will free you from some spell.

Your insolence taunts the king with malice.

Like you could drink from some Celtic chalice."

CLOVIS

"He is just a pilgrim on his own way.

Twelve years ago he and I had much to say.

He pacified Brittany for our gain.

Now we expand east and almost to Spain."

URSU

"Arthur offered peace to his whole domain.

But it came with much wasted blood and pain.

Do the Visi rule their Aquitaine home?

Tho' they had ignored the mantle of Rome."

CLOVIS

"At Vouille, I routed them in a day.

My lands are just short of the Narbonne spray.

Vandals still occupy the land you seek.

We are true Franks but speak Latin and Greek."

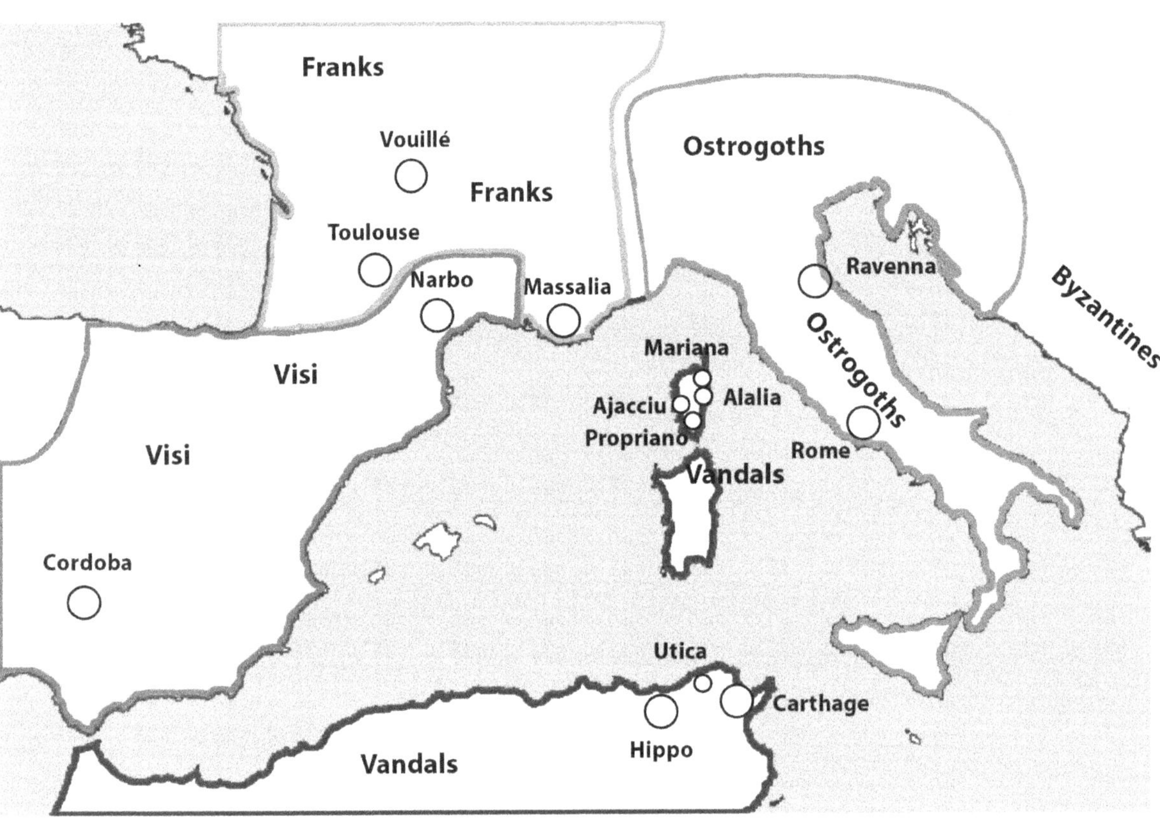

Frankish Expansion after the Battle of Voillé

**Ursu Finally Arrives at the Spring in the Village of Meria Where the End of His Long Quest
Has Brought Him to the Ancestral Town of Cor and Sica and to the Village Healer**

URSU

"The Vandals are strong without Rome's face.

They speak Latin but they neglect this place.

They care only for more wax, resin and wood.

They do not care for such springs as they should."

LA DONNA SIGNADORE

"Drink your fill as running water is good.

The serpent and God both drank as they could.

You have come far to where you do not know.

Yet, you feel each split terrace and rock row."

URSU

"I was not born in a village or town.

I have not run these paths both up and down.

I lack the local pathos in a song.

They all will know that I do not belong."

LA DONNA SIGNADORE

"Rome is not a shining city on a hill.

A village is not just bricks, stones or mill.

You are Corsican for you have the Grail.

You live true, fair, forthright and free so well."

URSU

"So, our village lives 'tho we were away.

It embraces us where we go far or stay.

I can go and find a new Frankish wife.

Our village supports me in joy and strife."

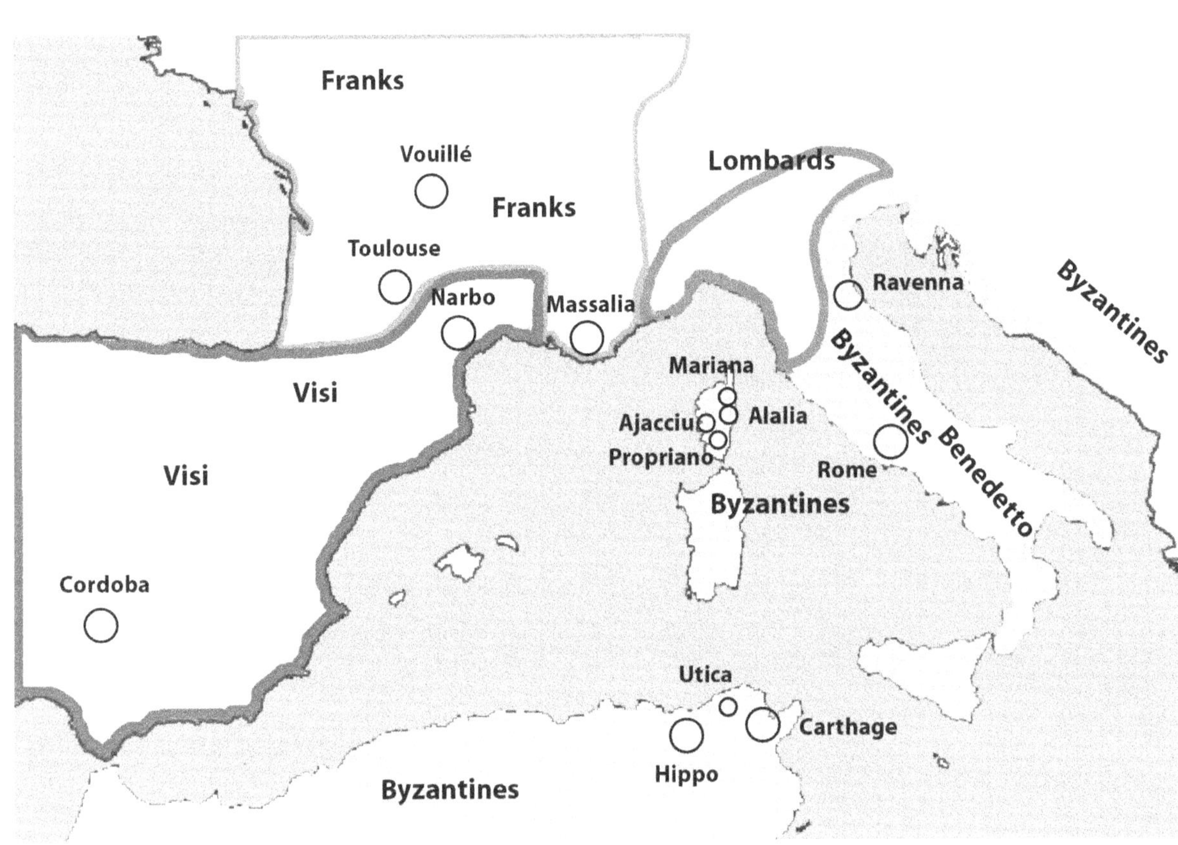

Byzantine Reconquest of the Western Roman Empire under the Emperor Justinian

Cyril the Byzantine Leader Arrives in the Port of Mariana and Ousts the Vandals – 535 CE

BRAVU

"The Vandal ships in the port are on fire.

Legions now swarm in glistening attire.

Ordered martialed strikes overrun the coast.

The sure precision would make anyone boast."

FIERU

"The Vandals fell like an old rotten tree.

But, do we have new bonds or are we free?

We all cannot resist such massive might.

Let us act without fear in their sight."

CYRIL

"The Vandal kingdom ends where it started.

Their rule is a gray ghost now departed.

Kyrnos again is part of mother Rome.

Go to your village or town that is home."

MEGALOFONOS

"Our Sea belongs to Rome from east to west.

Spain, North Africa, Italy and the rest.

I will stay as Prefect to rule without arms.

You will all return to your trade and farms."

CYRIL

"We are the Byzantine mask of Rome's face.

We do not seek to invade or displace.

Restore the rich commerce Phocis once found.

We will not long neglect you or the ground."

Pascal Paul Piazza

**The Corsicans Begin to Succumb to the Byzantine Tax Burden from
the Byzantine Authority in Carthage Necessary to Maintain the Far-Ranging
Byzantine Empire and Luxurious Living – 540 CE**

POMPIDOS

"After five years you would think you would learn.

The payment of taxes makes the world turn.

Carthage still needs more money for its debts.

I will take blood or flesh, but not regrets."

BRAVU

"Where is the freedom that Cyril did say?

Chains are re-forged in a different way!

Trade flourishes, yet that is not enough.

You force a new revolt as times are tough."

FIERU

"There will be a loud noise when the links break.

We will have to act for our family's sake.

You can take our honey, resin and wax.

Must we soon sell our sons to pay the tax?"

POMPIDOS

"That would be a good start to pay what's due.

That slaves make good money is very true.

It costs to run an empire for long.

Power requires wealth and not a song."

MEGALOFONOS

"I too must find monies for the coffers.

But, that is not what real freedom offers.

My fealty to my oath suffers in pain.

I fear revolt charges the air like rain."

JENIFER

"Look at our brothers and sisters right here.

Bleeding as the tax chain tightens each year.

The same pressure you and I have to bear.

The oppression so fueling fulsome fear."

CHJAMI AGHIALESI

"Let us stretch the links all together now.

Our earnest strength and fairness show us how.

Perhaps someday the brutal chain will break.

A roar will erupt as the ground will quake."

JENIFER

"Tell each village to remember the past.

And prepare for the future coming fast.

Our common ideas are a trenchant bond.

Holding us as one from each tree and pond."

CHJAMI AGHIALESI

"Let us stretch the links all together now.

Our forthright courage and love show us how.

How we live makes the unbreakable creed.

Being the true source of a brand-new seed."

JENIFER

"If we really want it then heed the call.

All hurdles before us will quickly fall.

Our roar is a song under the porches.

A chant of freedom lighting our torches."

Pascal Paul Piazza

King Totila and Teja, Both Ostrogoths, and Childeric, the Frank, Ally to Re-Take Corsica from the Byzantine Yoke – 540 CE

CHILDERIC

"Your light would welcome those here to save you.

As Ursu knew, we Franks mean freedom too.

We want this island to serve as our base.

From here, we will resist the Byzantine mace."

TEJA

"This land is beauty and should not suffer.

The Sea provides a defense and buffer.

We will make quick attacks where we are strong.

To secure redemption for every wrong."

TOTILA

"My kingdom has been reduced to this place.

I am still the projection of Rome's face.

Be safe in each coastal town and village.

We have come to build trade and not pillage."

BRAVU

"They look like Visi, but then again not.

A true Frank has such long hair in a knot.

How can there be freedom with a king?

This is not the path of the song we sing!"

FIERU

"Yet, they three come without troops on this day.

Leaving their army in ships on the bay.

Their bold conduct speaks louder than mere words.

I trust my heart not the entrails of birds."

CHILDERIC

"We know that the Chestnut staff steers us right.

Saints imbue wood, stone and courage to fight.

My father helped Ursu find his true way.

He indorses us to victory this day."

TOJA

"We are not the Visi to say the least.

We are cousin Goths that come from the east.

We saw the carnest young emperor fall.

We ruled in Latin from Ravenna's vast hall."

TOTILA

"Goth ambushed Goth to bring Theodoric's reign.

The mantle of Rome remained in the main.

He met the Visi, Vandal and Frank in peace.

Just as I hope your safety will not cease."

CHILDERIC

"He was a brilliant legate of the East.

Goths were Roman first and Gothic least.

His laws were fair to all women and men.

His scholars wrote with an insightful pen."

TOJA

"We fought with ourselves after he did pass.

Witiges restored peace in trade and Mass.

The Byzantine storm consumed our home land.

Now Totila is a true king that is grand."

TOTILA

"I will ambush Narses at Taginae.

That should keep the Byzantine force at bay.

I will leave some men to stop an assault.

You will be free to trade fresh meat with salt."

MEGALOFONOS

"How will you cruelly torture him and me?

Drop us like an anchor crossing the Sea?

Stone us on crosses in a village square?

Feed our liver to an eagle with care?"

CHILDERIC

"Those are all choices if we were a Greek.

We are the Roman virtue of the meek.

You will stay long and help govern for years.

He will enter a church and pray with tears."

TOJA

"It is time to restore roads, towns and walls.

We will tap the power of water falls.

Village and coast will each live as most choose.

You will have mainly peace unless we lose."

TOTILA

"This war is a slow tortured path for all.

We must resist for the eagle to fall.

It will be five years 'til we meet once more.

Goths and Franks march restively off to war."

**The Byzantine Eunuch General Narses Enters the Port of Mariana
To Restore Byzantine Hegemony Over Corsica from Carthage
with Overwhelming Force – 547 CE**

BRAVU

"Toja's broken boats enter the harbor.

Blood highlights the wooden deck beams' camber.

There are barely enough men to sail back.

Let us defend against the new attack."

FIERU

"You were gone so long we knew you had won.

We wanted to hear of deeds you had done.

Drink now and let us attend to your health.

You are home for good and now have your wealth."

TOJA

"Totila was struck like a lightning bolt.

Our army bolted like a restless colt.

For over four years we struggled in vain.

'Til our own bold blood covered us like rain."

NARSES

"Enough is enough the revolt must end.

Now is the true time to stay home and mend.

I have ships at every port with Greek fire,

Troops enough for towns to burn like a pyre."

MEGALOFONOS

"We clearly have heard the message you send.

Withdraw now as the weary war does end.

These are good people we cannot fleece.

I will rule for Carthage in equal peace."

Pascal Paul Piazza

Alboin and Rothari, Both Lombards (the New Rival Power in Northern Italy with the Byzantines in Ravenna) Enter the Marina of Meria on an Reconnaissance Mission – 585 CE

ALBOIN

"See if you can catch the long rope I cast.

I believe that I have broken my mast.

You can pull me into this welcome cove.

Its calm beach and woods are a treasure trove."

BELLEZZA

"Come around and dock slowly on the ground.

A new mast to install can soon be found.

I have never seen such long beards before.

Like some magical mystics from old lore."

ROTHARI

"We are just Lombards from across the sea.

We search for new near lands to know and see.

We now know Italy for twenty years.

We move around to stoke Ravenna's fears."

BELLEZZA

"It seems that no ship can resist this shore.

New and old tribes see and seem to want more.

Your mast is new and ready now to sail.

Stay for some food and drink as you look pale."

ALBION

"Thank you, but our wives will worry so soon.

We must return before the rise of the moon.

I can see why Rome fought hard for this place.

We will want to expand into this space."

CHAPTER SEVENTEEN

The Roman Now Gothic Quintet: The Last Foundation Stones Laid – 650 – 1000 CE

TASH

"A new faith explodes on the Sea stage.

Conquering lands like turning a new page.

Lines soon had to cross in a wholesale fight.

Cultures would clash just as day follows night."

PATTI

"Protection would change the face of the land.

Power renamed villages with a new brand.

Counts in the southwest laid an estate plan.

Oppressing new peasants as best they can."

BERNADETTE

"The face of Rome continues to change.

Spheres of influence move and rearrange.

Lombards and Franks usher in a new reign.

What was once old is holy and new again."

MARY

"Freedom arose to lifts its standard high.

The Commune gave voice to the lowly sighs.

Foes were struck hard and began then to dread.

Symbols strike on a white flag with Moor's head."

CHARLOTTE

"Peace would follow fast under Pisa's guise.

Roads, churches and trade would soon again rise.

Papal words inspire deeds in a great tale.

Leading to the duty of cross and mail."

**The Byzantine Leaders in Carthage Arrive in the Port of Mariana After
Defeat by the Muslim Forces and On Their Way to Administer Corsica from Ravenna
and Bring Musa the Berber on His Way Home – 695 CE**

CHJARU

"The six Byzantine ships barely made port.

The afternoon sun though tends to distort.

This is not the scene of imperial might.

But waves of beaten troops after a fight."

RITIRATU

"This bodes ill for a land under their rule.

When Carthage flees like a shark pursued school.

It is time I withdraw to my village.

I do not want to witness the pillage."

ALEXIOS

"The Exarchate of Carthage is no more.

Islam soon holds North Africa's shore.

As Prefect, I seek out Ravenna's Hall.

To discuss what other land may soon fall."

HERAKLEIOS

"They swarmed like locusts of an ancient test.

They leapt the wall and took the rest.

The East has long recalled my best defense.

Our known weakness made our lives very tense."

MUSA

"In sixty years, they came from unknown sands.

Now, they own Carthage to the holy lands.

They soon will invade my own Berber land.

Dihya will be there to make a strong stand."

ALEXIOS

"We must defend this island if we can.

They will soon target each woman and man.

No ship may pass without wanting to stay.

We must look to do it in your own way."

HERAKLEIOS

"We have less than a tenth of a legion.

We can barely protect this sole region.

We have no navy to patrol the shore.

But we have seasoned men brave to the core."

MUSA

"I will return home to fight hand to hand.

Freedom has been the hallmark of our land.

We will keep the trade route open and free.

There will be long support across the Sea."

CHJARU

"Coast towns are not like the cities back East.

They are not plums to pick upon and feast.

They can be easily left for the hills.

And which can resist the best martial skills."

RITIRATU

"High mountains passes deploy like bent rays.

Segmentally linking long valley ways.

Our feuds give way when there is a new foe.

These walls protect us from the winds that blow."

The Berbers Converted to Islam and Supplied the Main Army that Occupied Most of Spain by 711 CE. In the Great Hall in Cordoba, Musa and Tariq, Both Berbers, Warn Not to Attack Corsica – 713 CE

AL ABD JABBAR

"Al Andalus shines like the Spanish sun.

New fruit, food and crops trace this Arab run.

Two years have now gone since we won this place.

We should now expand both ideas and space."

MUSA

"You forget that Berbers mainly won this prize.

An Arab's crown face is a fake disguise.

The Visi were weak, but the Franks are not.

Their defense is a more difficult knot."

TARIQ

"We may be converts for just sixteen years.

But the truth faith of Allah in us sears.

We should attack the south coast of the Franks.

While maintaining trade with Corsica's ranks."

AL AB JABBAR

"We attack Cyrnos to occupy that place.

We will try to wipe out that wretched race.

They have not seen such a fight on the waves.

We will find wood, resin and many slaves."

MUSA

"We do not counsel such a reaction.

It is a mistaken and rash action.

You want their resin, wax and honey.

But the bee will save the hive not money."

Arabs Joined By Berbers First Attack Corsica Above the Port of Ajacciu – 713 CE

CHJARU

"It has been sixteen years without a fight.

We have not seen a Muslim ship in sight.

I fear that now something just is not right.

Tho' the sun is high and its rays are bright."

RITIRATU

"The glare hides two ships anchored offshore.

There may be up to at least fourteen more.

This may truly be a very dark day.

Sound the bell to see what passes this way."

AL ABD JABBAR

"Is there not one coward who fights us now?

Or is this island just a docile cow?

I came across the water for a fight.

Where is the supposed great Corsican might?"

IBN SAID

"We may never face a foe who is strong.

That there is nobody to beat us is wrong.

Their women will welcome some new real men.

When we cage these fake roosters as a hen."

CHJARU

"Our women would carve you like a fresh boar.

They wait for you two if you start this war.

My sword, shield and lance await a just fight.

Is there a worthy opponent in sight?"

RITIRATU

"We have prepared a long time for today.

Yet, I just hear the empty words you say.

We have done trade with the Berbers for years.

It is your choice of commerce or tears."

MUSA

"You four have fought for four hours on end.

It is clear what the message you each send.

You each bleed from open wounds that look grave.

You should each know that each of you is brave."

TARIQ

"The die is cast for an endless battle.

Dry drums will sound and swift swords will rattle.

There is no need to spill our blood right now.

Depart in honor exchanging a bow."

AL AB JABBAR

"You fight crudely but will some kind of skill.

I act now just because of Allah's will.

You are spared as a people of the Book.

I do not look half as bad as you look."

CHJARU

"My now lost Berber friends are wise with grace.

We need not bleed out at a harried pace.

Your skill with a sword is second to none.

But, I am sure that I still would have won."

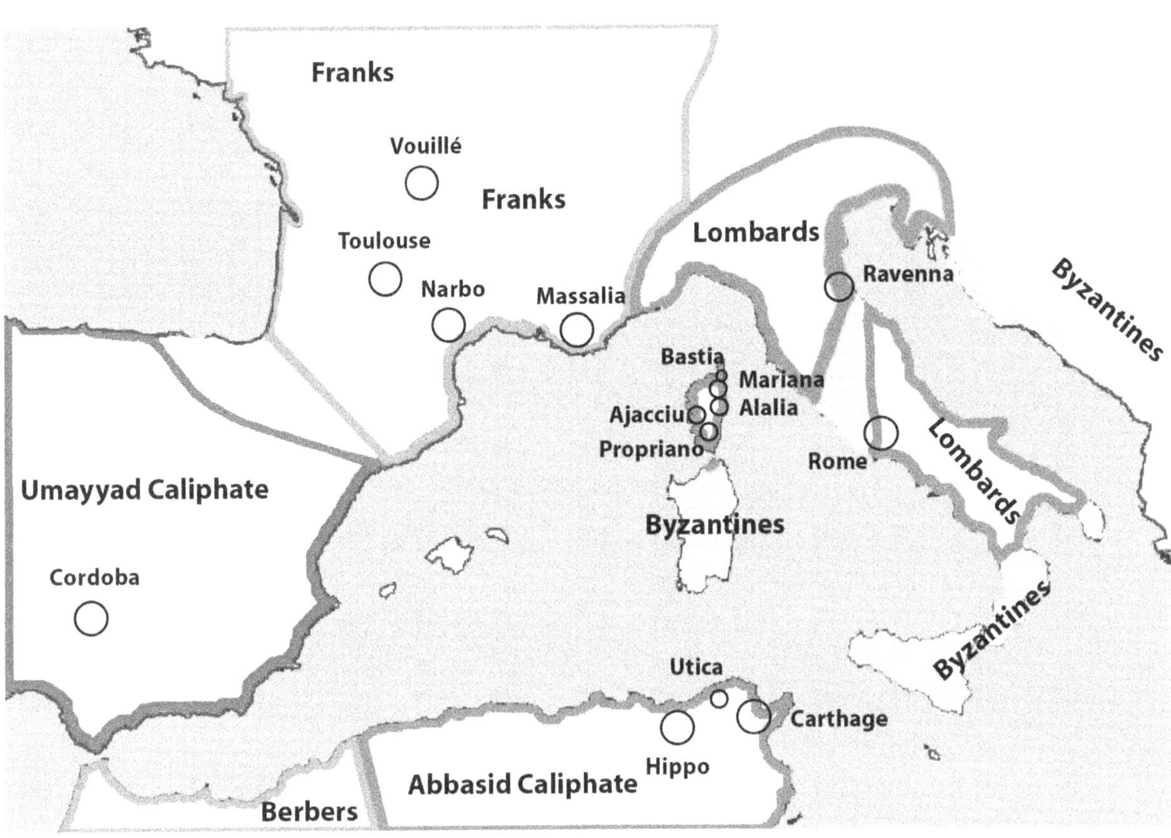

Maximum Extent of the Lombard Kingdom

**King Luitprand and Cleph of the Lombards and the Franks Arrive with an Army
at the Port of Meria to Drive Out the Muslims and Meet with Some Corsicans
Who Have not Withdrawn to the Maquis – 725 CE**

DRAGO

"The coastal towns were left since the first fight.

Trade blossoms with the Capu Corsu at night.

We arrange meetings at prearranged coves.

In between the Saracen attacks in droves."

TERZU

"The Moors well know of the Vandal's mistake.

When they see each Moor's head set on a stake.

We lack enough good troops to keep them away.

But, the mountain passes keep them at bay."

TENTAZIONE

"Still, they want women like me to be slaves.

My looks and skill are what the market craves.

Or help rule if we pay a certain price.

Lost troops to rule is a great sacrifice."

CLEPH

"The Moors hold some coast land to try to rule.

Their only true need though is the slave pool.

Land is held and then given back at least.

They feel few restraints on the coastal east."

LUITPRAND

"Our fight with the Greeks can wait one more day.

We Lombards will pay what we have to pay.

We cannot ignore this land in distress.

The Moors can no longer seek to oppress."

DRAGO

"I have not seen so many ships arrayed.

Even when Narses appeared and we all prayed.

Frank and Lombard boats too many to count.

There would be multiple severed heads to mount."

TERZU

"The Moors did not count on such an attack.

They had no redoubts in which to fall back.

They lack the armies to fight in two places.

And still suppress some other wide spaces."

TENTAZIONE

"The armies flowed like waves over the rocks.

Women set on supine stragglers with blocks.

They would not be slaves on any basis.

That practice was soon to be in stasis."

CLEPH

"The Moors had many converts to the cause.

Many could see good reasons now to pause.

The coastal towns could restore its vast trade.

Yet, they had fears or more Moors to invade."

LUITPRAND

"I am Rome where Ravenna cannot be.

I will surely watch from across the Sea.

But, the East and I have to fight each day.

I hope soon we all will return to stay."

**Charles Martel (the Hammer) and the Franks Along with Some Corsicans
Face the Muslim Onslaught in Gaul at the Battle of Tours and Establish
the Ascendency of the Carolingian Dynasty– 732 CE**

DRAGO

"Two years ago the Moors took Aquitaine.

Blood, charcoal and sulphur fell like black rain.

Soon the mainly Christian world could be lost.

It must be won at any and all cost."

TERZU

"We met Attila saving the world's fate.

We accept this burden 'tho it is great.

We will meet the Saracen on the field.

We will not stop, bend, break or ever yield."

TENTAZIONE

"Before, we held a baton of a boar.

It was our high standard to win a war.

Now, we hold a flag showing the Moor's head.

That we resolve to stand 'til they are dead."

CHARLES MARTEL

"The Moors hit first and found a steadfast wall.

Corsicans held never fearing to fall.

The day's fight saw Moor's loss of loot and life.

'Til they withdrew to Spain to avoid strife."

CHARLES MARTEL

"This was a hammer stroke for a rebirth.

Kings should only seek to build with true worth.

We will never forget our island friends.

Whose full fairness and freedom never ends."

Pascal Paul Piazza

Pope Stephen Meets King Aistulf of the Lombards in Pavia and Disputes Arise
Including the Administration of Corsica – 754 CE

POPE STEPHEN

"Three years ago Ravenna fell at last.

With no foe the Lombards expanded fast.

You have riches that must be sent to me.

It is time to swear fealty to the See."

AISTULF

"We seized power because I am now king.

You should bow low and kiss my golden ring.

How much tribute will you begin to pay?

Will you answer to me starting this day."

POPE STEPHEN

"I answer to no man but to our Lord.

He will tear you down by His fervent sword.

Pippin is chosen to wield it in life.

To cure your cold heathen soul from its strife."

AISTULF

"We are the Franks' allies for many years.

Moor heads adorn the end of many spears.

The Exarchate stood in Luitprand's way.

Now Corsica can be within our sway."

POPE STEPHEN

"You are like a restive wild unchained bear.

You must be sealed in your restless lair.

I will return with an army of light.

Tales will long be told about its awesome might."

Corsicans and Lombards Ally In the Port of Mariana – 754 CE

ALBOIN

"Will the Franks side with the Pope in battle?

If they do then the whole ground will rattle.

We can lose all the land that we just won.

All of our great gains may soon be undone."

AISTULF

"If they do, they will attack us at home.

Then they will try to seize some land near Rome.

We must enlist support in all our land.

A people's army so large and so grand."

TERZU

"You can start here as was Luitprand's great wish.

We come back to the coast to live and fish.

With your army the Moors will stay away.

I am sad the Franks are not here this day."

TENTAZIONE

"We will build villages along the Sea.

With the houses of families so free.

This is the face of Rome that had to be.

It is the place we all wanted to see."

ALBOIN

"This is Aistulf's kingdom, but it is your home.

We bring a small army that will not roam.

We must leave as the Pope may get his way.

If he does it will be a bloody day."

Pascal Paul Piazza

Pope Stephen Enlists King Pippin of the Franks at the Abbey of St. Denis Outside Paris to Attack the Lombards Who Have Been Long Allies of the Franks– 754 CE

PIPPIN

"You should stay the winter to salve your soul.

We have plenty of good food, drink and coal.

You dislike my friend who fought at my side?

How can I leave him and retain any pride?"

POPE STEPHEN

"The Franks have been chosen to serve our Lord.

To rid the menace of the Lombard horde.

I will anoint you king above the rest.

But you just have to pass this simple test."

PIPPIN

"I was chosen king two years in the past.

By the vote of warriors meant to last.

We have been Catholics for many years.

My strong devotion is not in arrears."

POPE STEPHEN

"It is time Rome's Church and king be as one.

Just as the Father is the same as the Son.

You will give me vast estates around Rome.

And rights to rule Corsica as my home."

PIPPIN

"I will tell Aistulf that you are his liege.

This is not the time to make war or siege.

He will want to meet at a holy place.

He can make peace or die at his pace."

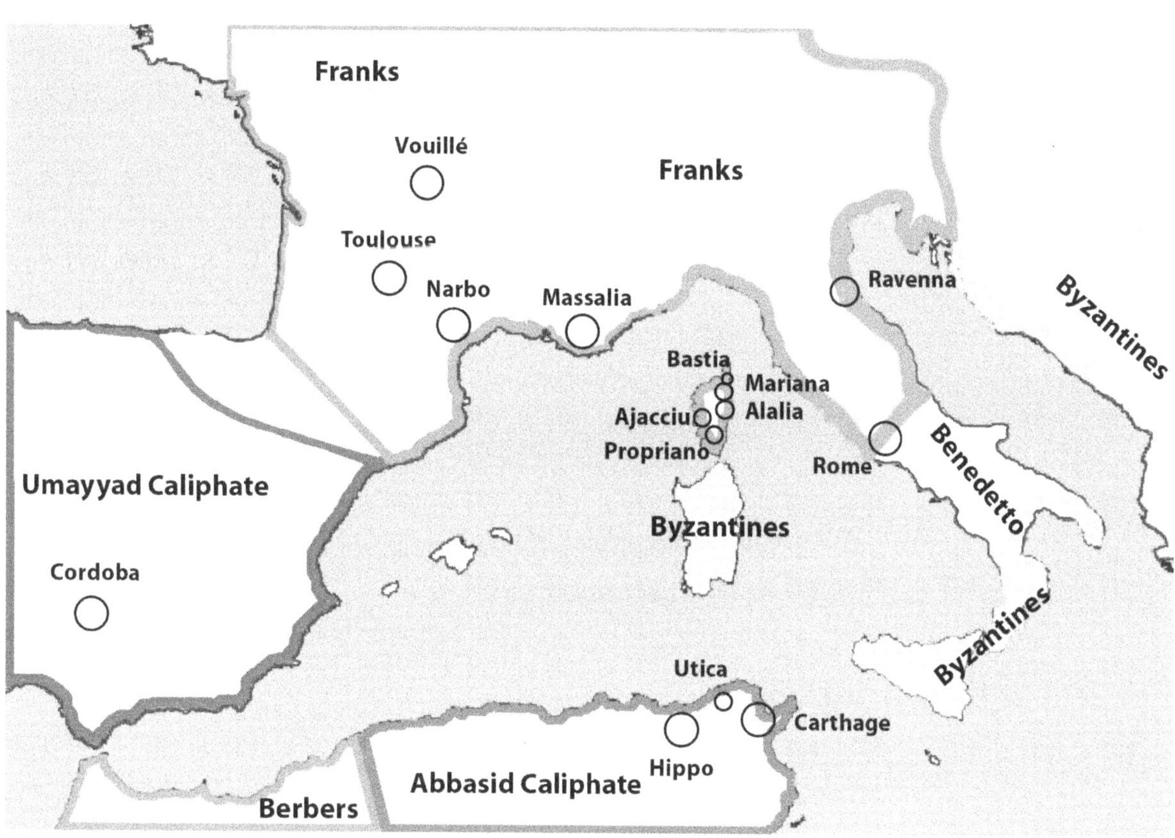

Frankish-Roman Empire of Charlemagne

Pascal Paul Piazza

Pippin's Son Charles Defeats the Lombards Who Withdraw to Corsica Which Has Now Been Annexed to the Frankish Kingdom – 774 CE

MARZIALE

"More Lombard ships and fresh troops dock this day.

Our defenses grow stronger in each way.

Boats can patrol the coast stopping attacks.

Wagons and men follow any Moorish tracks."

PRUDENZIA

"More backs to build better baths and bridges.

New roads for farmers among the ridges.

Larger bins to store crops to trade afar.

Tall towers with a torch just like a star."

THURISIND

"We have come to make this land our new home.

We had to journey across the white foam.

Aistulf chose not to concede to the Pope.

He then died at the end of Pippin's rope."

LIUTPERT

"Pippin and the Pope both chose the next king.

As we fought ourselves to wear the chief's ring.

Desidarius won back all our lands.

Peace was then held squarely in our own hands."

ARIPERT

"He just lost to Charles who is Pippin's son.

Who has annexed all our land that he won.

Charles is king of the Franks and Lombards too.

Making him now Corsica's liege so true."

**The Lombards Bring an Unknown Shi'a Persian Muslim Captive Who is an Abbasid
from Carthage and Different Than the Umayyads Ruling in Spain.
Both Abbasid and Umayyad Seek to Attack Corsica.**

MARZIALE

"Franks and Lombards have long been our allies.

Forming one reign like this is a surprise.

You will live with us wherever you like.

Just so long you watch for the next Moor strike."

PRUDENZIA

"You have a captive that is new to me.

He looks like a Persian lost on the Sea.

He is not like the Berber or Arab foe.

He has sown the sole seeds of his own woe."

QADI AL MANSUR

"By Allah's own will which alone is great.

From Baghdad I am here to seal my fate.

From Carthage I strike the infidel's land.

Blessing from the Abbasid Caliph's hand."

THURISIND

"He was left by a Moorish fleet at sea.

God's mercy brought him quickly before me.

The old Umayyads now rule mainly Spain.

The Abbasids hold court from Carthage's plain."

LIUTPERT

"It seems Muslims in-fight just as we do.

He should live because our honor is true.

We fight Muslims tribes from our south and west.

We should go inland where our strength is best."

Pascal Paul Piazza

**Lombards and Corsicans Are at Home in Corsica and Celebrate Midnight Mass
in the Village of Meria and Proceed to their Homes in the Villages in
the Mountains Through Candles – December 24, 800 CE**

ARIPERT

"The night chill freshly brings hope to my face.

Child-red cheeks find a happiness to trace.

We have come to find this village is home.

We have truly found the mantle of Rome."

MARZIALE

"Our village is our paese and heart.

Tonight, we follow where the candles start.

From church down the path to a fired stove.

From Midnight Mass to our own treasure trove."

PRUDENZIA

"All our flames match the stars in the night sky.

An obsidian black blanket set so high.

Folk songs and laughter combust the cold air.

Hope captures this festival of the fair."

PANATTERU

"We come from Patinu and Carucu.

We are our aunts, uncles, and cousins too.

Rock passes are arteries for our blood.

We combine now for our family flood."

VENDITORE

"We own our land and we work with our hands.

We bring bread, honey and meat from our lands.

We share an oath to be forthright and free.

This is our guidance from mountain and Sea."

**The Next Day, and Also Through Candles, Pope Leo Crowns King Charles
the Great (Charlemagne) in Rome as the Ruler and Defender
of the Restored Roman-Frankish Empire – December 25, 800 CE**

EINHARD

"Two rows of candles ignite a new morn.

The cohesion of the West is reborn.

He now holds from the Ebro to the Rhine.

From St. Omer's fields to Amalfi's wine."

ZACHARIUS

"I come with two keys from His Holy Grave.

The East's tribute with fulsome grace to save.

No new emperor now sits in the East.

We shall find one to sit from today's feast."

POPE LEO

"He is the peacemaker by God's grace.

Saving the Church from the whole heathen race.

Here is the Frank-Lombard king in the West.

He is most serene august Charles the Best."

KING CHARLEMAGNE

"My crown weighs much, but not from its metal.

It asks whether I possess the mettle.

I watch my lands like a shepherd its flock.

I hold the keys to the eternal lock."

BONIFACE

"I accept your staff for the Tuscan march.

The true vanguard of the Ligurian arch.

We will protect Cyrnos as it was done.

Until the war against the Moor is won."

Pascal Paul Piazza

Charlemagne's Cionstable Burchard and the Tuscan Boniface Rescue 500 Corsican Slaves (Including Schiavu, Opaca, Dolore and Liberu) Aboard Moorish Ships Off the Capu Corsu – 806 CE

SCHIAVU

"Most of the five hundred knew just the land.

The salt spray made tight the rope on each hand.

None had sought to make a trip on the waves.

They had once been free, but now they were slaves."

OPACA

"Moors take all but the old, infirm or dead.

Sixty-two in each boat not to be fed.

Set for the high Andalus auction house.

All will be sold and split even each spouse."

DOLORE

"The open air breathes the cruelest unknown.

What lay ahead can ripple like sails blown.

We have been sold as solvent slaves before.

The concept though crushes our very core."

LIBERU

"Ships arise out of the glare of the sun.

A vast fleet of hope forces the Moors to run.

Their cargo is a weight that slows their pace.

Their less numbers fall with blood on the face."

BURCHARD

"Your captors are dead or on a ship back.

They will know it is folly to attack.

Our oath is to protect the island's shore.

But, the Saracen still returns for more."

BONIFACE I

"Moors creep from Spain and Persians from the south.

Imbued with passion from an Imam's mouth.

They raid just to show sometimes that they can.

A coast too long to post each island man."

SCHIAVU

"We shall heed what the caporali said.

Or else we too will soon end up so dead.

We seek the shield of the valley and pass.

Leaving the shore alone to Moors so crass."

OPACA

"Saracens are split very far and wide.

Fighting each other, Greeks and Franks aside.

They soon tire to not expose a side.

And not lose a kingdom or their pride."

DOLORE

"Moors will not rest if there are docks and wax.

They seek gain by plunder and not by tax.

Today, they lost eight ships and many slaves.

Yet, their ships swarm like bees over the waves."

LIBERU

"But, we are free absolved from our mistake.

It is our indolence that we must forsake.

We plan to let them wash over our shore.

While Charles' wooden fleets settle the score."

Pascal Paul Piazza

In Rome, Pope Stephen IV Enlists Roman Counts Higo Colonna, Cirnarca Colonna and Guido Savelli and the Disgraced Ganelon to Attack the Moors in Corsica in Exchange for Estates There – 816 CE

POPE STEPHEN IV

"God gives us a gift from his Holy grace.

Spill Moor blood and end your own past disgrace.

Eject Muslims and found your own estate.

Create a band of counts for a new state."

HUGO COLONNA

"The young Charles routed the Moors six years past.

That great success would not very long last.

For two years Abbasids consumed one coast.

The emir repeats his bellow and boast."

CIRNARCA COLONNA

"The Great Charles died quickly two years ago.

The rule of his sons is moving quite slow.

No leader arises to seize his true sword.

We do so now and land is our reward."

GANELON

"My house's stain seems set like a die is cast.

Yet, its course must break the chains of the past.

Muslim blood welcomes a brand-new rebirth.

We will celebrate with such joy and mirth."

GUIDO SAVELLI

"We nobles of Rome uphold its tablets.

We carry them on the path the sun sets.

The caporali wait with troops onboard.

Desperate for one to wield the true sword."

Count Bera of Barcelona Joins Hugo Colonna, Cirnarca Colonna, Guido Savelli and Ganelon Outside Mariana to Fight Nugalon Emir of Corsica – 818 CE

BERA - COUNT OF BARCELONA

"The Pope secured our seven hundred men.

To help provide you with another win.

Your campaign proceeds without its full prize.

Now it is time for the pressure to rise."

A MUSLIM ASTROLOGER

"I walk from Mariana's fort this morn.

Each grey whisker in my beard is forlorn.

The omens are ill, many and discrete.

The signs prefigure a Muslim defeat."

CIRNARCA COLONNA

"Our armies deploy outside the fort.

Both sides in counterpoise outside the port.

Hubris huffs haughtily from the whole hosts.

`Nostrils flare like beasts loosed from the posts."

HUGO COLONNA

"I kiss the cross on my sword for its grace.

The will of our God occupies this place.

A pure win on this field has been ordained.

The oath of our true faith has been maintained."

HUGO COLONNA

"There is a just war and this must be it.

Remission of sins follows with each hit.

If you die, you join the Angels on high.

And live in Elysian fields in the sky."

NUGALONE - EMIR OF MARIANA AND ALERIA

"I twist my moustache as I have no fear.

Allah alone wills what will happen here.

He is great and He animates the wind.

His message is one I alone can send."

NUGALONE - EMIR OF MARIANA AND ALERIA

"This is jihad and our cause must be just.

We but serve Him with our aim that we trust.

If you die you all Baghdad will rejoice.

Forever live with the virgins of choice."

GANELON

"Hugo moved strongly with a tiger's grace.

The emir countered with a panther's pace.

I held the front line wiping clean my slate.

Cirnarca protected his brother's fate."

GUIDO SAVELLI

"This was a field of honor and heart.

But blood flowed freely from the very start.

Mutual respect was soon built with each loss.

Even if it were for the crescent or cross."

BERA - COUNT OF BARCELONA

"The field was won when the emir withdrew.

This would be a fight someday to renew.

The Pope made counts as he said he would make.

Each leader chose a vast estate to take."

Adelbert, Son of Boniface II (Who Founded the Fortress of Bonifacio on the Southern Tip), and Berard Pledge the Tuscan March to Defend Corsica – 846 CE

ADLEBERT

"Our father, Boniface, founded this fort.

To guard the Straight and to trade from this port.

Our shear high rock walls cannot be broken.

A seal that our fealty is not a token."

BERARD

"Thirteen years past, there was a sea battle.

That made stone docks of Utica rattle.

The Abbasid ships withdrew during the night.

Ceding the bright day to our father's might."

ADELBERT

"The coast remains a fluid in attack

The Moor leaves, but still returns soon to sack.

No defeat of the Muslim is certain.

Tho' father tore down the Persian curtain."

BERARD

"The people stay high above the war fray.

Counts offer some solace in their own way.

They take lands acting like a lawful liege.

And offer protection from any Muslim siege."

ADELBERT

"We are the true invested Count without tiers.

Lucca's men met the oath to guard for years.

Corsica was ceded to Middle France.

The Tuscan March wields here both shield and lance."

Pascal Paul Piazza

**Adelbert Retires in Autun and Meets with Conrad, Son of the Holy Roman Emperor Otto I,
Debating Adalbert's Attacks from Corsica Against Otto and the Empire's
Later Defense of Corsica – 965 CE**

ADALBERT

"We have spent more time in-fighting than most.

I am not sure that is something to boast.

Our pure island mandate remained unchanged.

But, the coast's land kept being exchanged."

CONRAD

"New Fatimid raids came before your reign.

Three distinct Muslims sought the island plain.

Arabs built a fort at St. Tropez's shore.

Our long absence let them gain so much more."

ADALBERT

"Berengar and I were Italy's kings.

Forced on knees to kiss each of Otto's rings.

Brought down because of a young women's rage.

We each only had war against Otto to wage."

CONRAD

"You spent time in the Arab pirates' fort.

Then twice Corsica became your home port.

Launching new campaigns of every sort.

But each time you soon had to abort."

ADALBERT

"Otto's Rome assumed the old Tuscan role.

Leaving to the Luccas the island's soul.

Counts and villagers soon had to collide.

Greed and fear conflict with fair freedom's pride."

**Sambucuccio Leads the Villagers Against the Counts Led by Count Cirnarca to
Prevent the Counts from Occupying All of Corsica and Extending
Their Brutal Oppression of the Villagers – 1000 CE**

SAMBUCUCCIO

"You shall not have our triangle of land.

For the Terra del Commune we now stand.

Our line goes from Aleria to Calvi.

And then to rocky Brandu on the Sea."

COUNT CIRNARCA

"God's grace calls for larger estates of land.

Like in France, Lombardy and the Rhineland.

Serfs seek to serve well and make us much money.

Gone are the days of wheat, wax, meat and honey."

SAMBUCUCCIO

"You have turned the true order on its side.

Being free and fair succumb to greed and pride.

Land, want and savage nature make us one.

That equality cannot be undone."

COUNT CIRNARCA

"The flags of all nine counts flow in the wind.

Hardened troops have a strong message to send.

We have our divine rights second to none.

The new social order needs to be won."

SAMBUCUCCIO

"We have free farmers, herders and coopers.

Fighting for their home unlike your troopers.

Swarming like bees, but not for some cold crest.

But, to save the comb of life that is best."

COUNT CIRNARCA

"I am lord which I have earned by my birth.

There is order by rank and perceived worth.

Villagers support me and know their place.

They all stay in line by brute force and mace"

SAMBUCUCCIO

"We are a commonwealth of the land.

Votes reflect each parish, village and hand.

Padri are there to protect all from harm.

Caporale serve to sound an alarm."

COUNT CIRNARCA

"I need no group to make a decision.

I need no debate or frank derision.

I need no help to make up my own mind.

I need little aid from masses so blind."

SAMBUCUCCIO

"Villages choose a Podesta for one year.

To serve as prefects sowing good not fear.

Podestas elect twelve then to rule and reign.

To pass new laws and to end your campaign."

COUNT CIRNARCA

"You join as one to rule and now to die.

There is no peace to be made if we try.

Prepare now for full combat to the end.

We will not wholly falter, break or bend."

SAMBUCUCCIO

"His troops think we will break upon attack.

So when they engage let us first fall back.

We will engulf them like a mad bull's horns.

And pierce them like the mountain sticker thorns."

COUNT CIRNARCA

"Hit them hard like the poor peasants down south.

They will bolt when they taste blood in the mouth.

You will be a phalanx of fear and might.

They will quickly start running from your sight."

SAMBUCUCCIO

"Hold firm and stick strictly to the war plan.

Use their mass against them as we now can.

Swarm like mad bees whose hive is on fire.

Entrap them in our set net and mire."

COUNT CIRNARCA

"They have not broken and stand resolute.

We have no new tactic to institute.

We make the same mistake as Cannae's field.

It is time to withdraw and to yield."

SAMBUCUCCIO

"Cirnarca left the field without remorse.

He seeks now to return home with his horse.

The battle is over and he has lost.

We mourn the dead and honor their great cost."

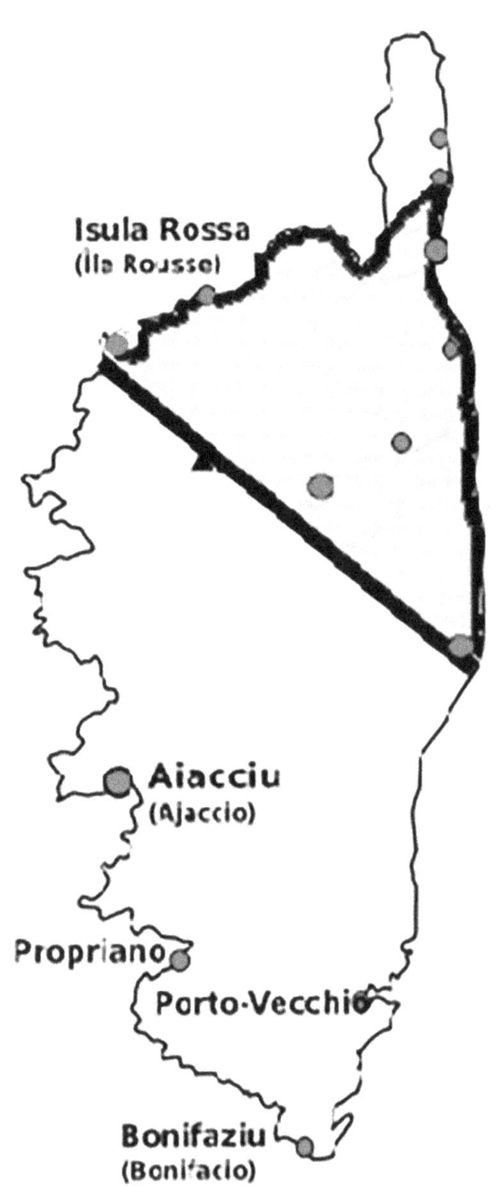

TERRA DEL COMMUNE

***The Terra Del Commune Supplied Representative Government Outside the realms
of the Counts. After Sambucuccio's Death, the Counts Try to Regain Power
But Are Stopped by the Tuscan Malaspina - 1112 CE***

PRAGMATICU

"For some twelve years, the Commune flourished.

Our fairness and free spirit were nourished.

A true model republic could exist.

Mapping how in the future to subsist."

ARRABBIATU

"Our leader has died and the counts arise.

Waging war and cruelty to no surprise.

What good is our union at a spear's point?

Our pure soul cannot fix a broken joint."

MALASPINA

"Do not despair for your current bad plight.

We accept your invitation to fight.

We land active troops up and down the shore.

And when we need them, we will call for more."

PRAGMATICU

"The counts have had years to plan to return.

They extract revenge on wheat fields they burn.

They seek to starve us into giving up.

They want us to have to drink from their cup."

ARRABBIATU

"They will not make the same mistakes as before.

They are all thirsting for a bloody war.

There are many more counts since we last fought.

Feudal lands grow as soon as they are bought."

MALASPINA

"We relish a robust round with the rebels.

Align the flags, the coat mail and symbols.

We will never wait for them to attack.

They will never know what is front and back."

OBERTO

"I will hit Gentili after he left home.

I will sack his lands as the Goths did Rome.

He will return to the Capu Corsu.

To a trap by which for peace he must sue."

ALBERTO

"Ganelon's heirs still bear family shame.

I will show that their character still is lame.

I will rout them before they can report.

Death will join cowardice as their consort."

MALASPINA

"Cirnarca will have to fight on his own.

His bluster is like the winds that have blown.

His hubris is an empty hollow shell.

He should listen for the pealing death knell."

OBERTO

"Let us deploy and accomplish our tasks.

We will soon drink the best wine from old casks.

Freedom is now ready to fuel the soul.

It time to lift the people from their hole."

The Pisans Unexpectedly Arrive to Route the Muslims at the Port at Mariana - 1170 CE

ONESTU

"The Commune was secure after eight years.

For fifty more it was salve for all fears.

But, now Muslim ships again fill the port.

Our Tuscans will not last in their old fort."

GHJUSTU

"Raise the call for local troops to arrive.

If we attack now we just may survive.

But wait, Pisan ships block the ships at dock.

Greek fire covers most sails, wood and rock."

JACAPO CURINI

"We were deployed to stop the Muslim force.

They have lost as a matter of due course.

Troops disembark to bolster the defense.

We and the Tuscans make a wall so dense."

ONESTU

"Welcome and thanks for your timely advance.

We could not stand another Moorish trance.

Most people shelter in the maquis high.

Our ports are home for the sea birds that fly."

GHJUSTU

"My brother exaggerates on one hand.

Yet, the Moors have forced us to go inland.

Tuscan fealty served for two hundred years.

Saving us from the burden of our tears."

Pascal Paul Piazza

**Pope Gregory the Great and Bishop Landulph of Pisa Discuss the Donation of Corsica
to the Pope and the Full Transfer of the Administration of Corsica to Pisa
Over Genoa's Objection – 1174 CE**

POPE GREGORY THE GREAT

"The Franks gave us the island as our lands.

We have ignored her, but our right still stands.

The Tuscans serve as legate to the Pope.

We now wish to restore order and hope."

BISHOP LANDULPH OF PISA

"Pisan troops have restored peace in four years.

The people greet these men with gifts and cheers.

I blessed them in your name when they left home.

The island's beauty asks them not to roam."

POPE GREGORY THE GREAT

"Thus, I tell you to leave without delay.

Find out what the six bishops there may say.

Do they look to the Luccas or to Rome?

Where do they find their true spiritual home?"

BISHOP LANDULPH OF PISA

"Genoa will protest Pisa's full role.

A Pope's word cannot change like his stole.

Pisa lost lives keeping the Muslims at bay.

The unclean heathen has long gone away."

POPE GREGORY THE GREAT

"Pisa will reign if the bishops concur.

Genoa's own claim will have to demur.

They may still appoint a bishop or three.

But Pisa will be the legate for me."

**The Pisans and Corsicans Debate Pisan Rule After the Great Schism,
the Turkish Win at Manzikert and How the Corsicans Remain Corsicans Under Pisan Rule
Which Has Been Fair and Just – 1092 CE**

ORLANDO OF PISA

"Pisa has ruled since your bishops agreed.

Eighteen short years to start to sow the seed.

Fights among counts and the Commune did cease.

God's Truce led to the nascent Pisan Peace."

BISHOP LANDULPH OF PISA

"Pope Urban now confirms Pisa as lord.

Genoa will defer and put down its sword.

Yes, Pisa shall govern this feudal fief.

This Papal Bull guarantees quick relief."

ONESTU

"Pisan rule has been fair, honest and true.

They have just done what they said they would do.

We can return from the maquis to thrive.

This island will be robustly alive."

GHJUSTU

"Our trade will reconnect to the Great Sea.

The spread of goods will show that we are free.

We assume the position we used to hold.

The center of commerce so frank and bold."

RETTITUDINE

"These men still dream as if they are asleep.

They ignore the price we pay that is steep.

Pisa may be lord, but not of our soul.

We remain free with the land as a whole."

MODESTU

"That the island is its women is clear.

They compose each other without a peer.

You seek to control with decisions made.

Immutably, we will cut with a blade."

ORLANDO OF PISA

"We came to help, but not subjugate, you.

We can build respect and make money too.

The Great Sea explodes with trade in the East.

Normans should not be alone at that feast."

BISHOP LANDULPH OF PISA

"Christ's Church split almost forty years ago.

The menace of Muslim Turks will still grow.

We need churches here to shepherd the flock.

To build as St. Peter did block by block."

RETTITUDINE

"Acts not clever words supply the true test.

My hands will tell me what is right and best.

Churches, roads, bridges and ports are just fine.

We need seeds for wheat and grapes for the wine."

MODESTU

"In all, we are free and never had slaves.

We attract each ship sailing on the waves.

You can change a standard, flag, name or crest.

But, fairness, faith and freedom still must vest."

Bishop Landulph of Pisa Carries the Crusading Message from Pope Urban II Preached on November 18, 1095 and Once Again Corsicans Take Up a Cause to be Honest and Just – June 1096 CE

BISHOP LANDULPH OF PISA

"The Pope preached a crusade last November.

They say it was a speech to remember.

Pisa stocks our ports for the ships to come.

We must confront the Moor and not be mum."

ONESTU

"Why should I travel when the Moor comes here?

That we have fought more Moors before is clear.

Three types of Muslims have tried to kill me.

The fourth Turk can remain across the Sea."

BISHOP LANDULPH OF PISA

"You must strike the unholy infidel first.

Before the heathen Turk gets the blood thirst.

Strike in the way that Malaspina did.

Box them all in with a true strangling lid."

GHJUSTU

"Turks come from the steppes like many before.

Yes, their first act is to engage in war.

But, they are just seeking to find a home.

And no longer have to migrate or roam."

BISHOP LANDULPH OF PISA

"There are too many people in the West.

A wandering back East is for the best.

We need God's Truce to stop the killing here.

Civil wars help the Saracen we fear."

O N E S T U

"We will go from a village to each port.

There are still not enough to man each fort.

The Commune has been God's Truce in action.

Pisa has overcome each prior faction."

B I S H O P   L A N D U L P H   O F   P I S A

"The Muslim defiles our holiest places.

Pilgrims are found with blood on their faces.

We must oust the Moor with a total win.

And you will receive remission of sin."

G H J U S T U

"We do what is fair, honest and forthright.

God does not bribe us to do what is right.

The ram, boar and bear rise to do their best.

When our essence embodies each such quest."

B I S H O P   L A N D U L P H   O F   P I S A

"The Pope noted the need for just such men.

Those who aid others again and again.

You are the vanguard to reverse the loss.

Wear proudly now the white vest with red cross."

O N E S T U

"We will go east as Babu did before.

But, we will go there to conduct a war.

We will not kill for spite, hate or for pride.

A new vest will not change us much inside."

TIME TABLE

1   CORSICA
EUROPE RELATED TO CORSICA
NEOLITHIC
Transition
6,000 BCE   Carnac
Megalithic   Hunting/Gathering
Filitosa   Cauria Zone   to   4,000 BCE   Alignments
Herding
Dolmens   Fontanaccia   to Trans-Humance
Alignment   Palaggiu   to
Santari   Cultivation
Renaughju   to
Villages
Minoans
Cist Tombs
Chalcolithic   3,000 BCE   Stonehenge
Bronze   LMNC Zone   Punic Zone   1,800 BCE
1,600 BCE   Mycenaeans   Etruscans
Torrean   Filitosa   Sherden   Phoenicians   1,500 BCE
(new stones)
Celts-Gauls
Filitosa   1,200 BCE
(new stones)   1180 BCE   Troy Falls
1177 BCE
814 BCE   Carthage Founded   Carthaginians
First Cities   810 BCE
753 BCE   Rome Founded
Romans
Iron Age   700 BCE

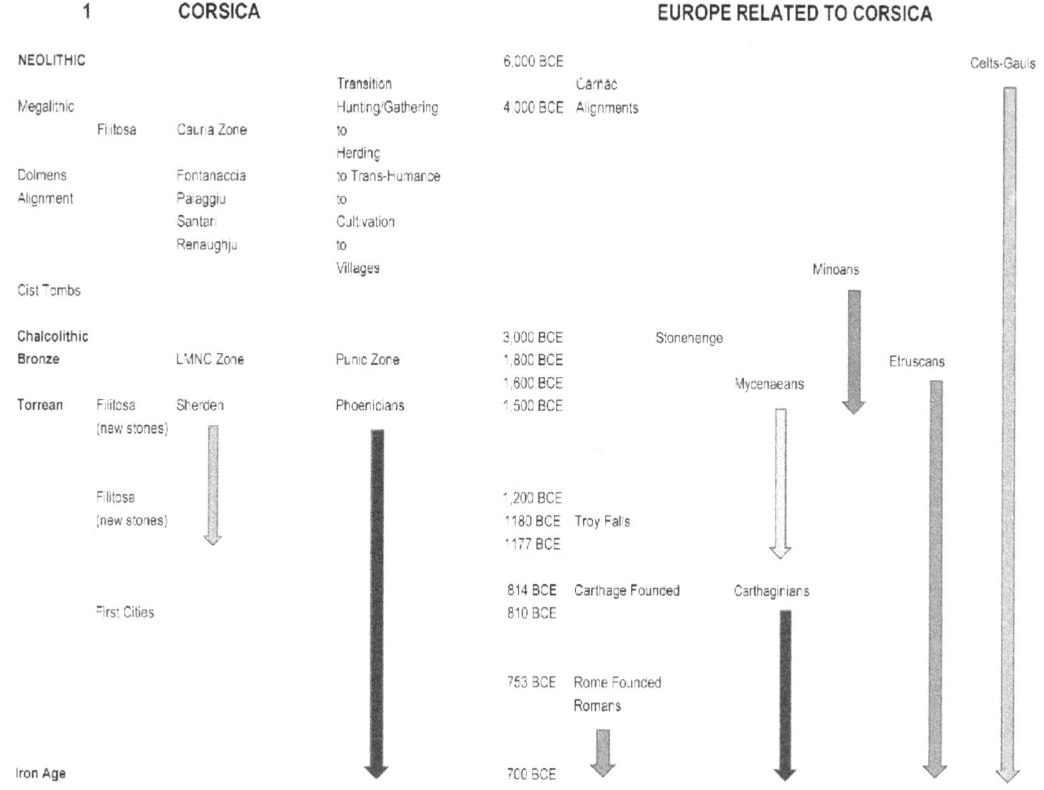

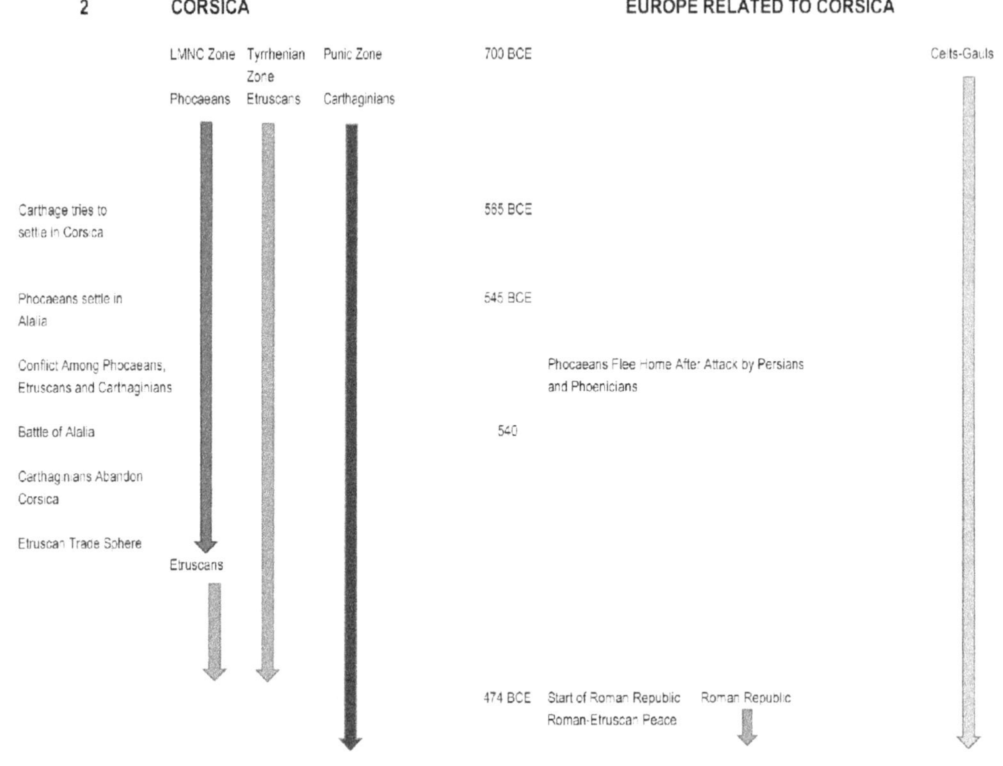
2   CORSICA
EUROPE RELATED TO CORSICA
LMNC Zone   Tyrrhenian   Punic Zone
Zone
Phocaeans   Etruscans   Carthaginians
700 BCE
Celts-Gauls
Carthage tries to
settle in Corsica
585 BCE
Phocaeans settle in
Alalia
545 BCE
Conflict Among Phocaeans,
Etruscans and Carthaginians
Phocaeans Flee Home After Attack by Persians
and Phoenicians
Battle of Alalia
540
Carthaginians Abandon
Corsica
Etruscan Trade Sphere
Etruscans
474 BCE   Start of Roman Republic   Roman Republic
Roman-Etruscan Peace

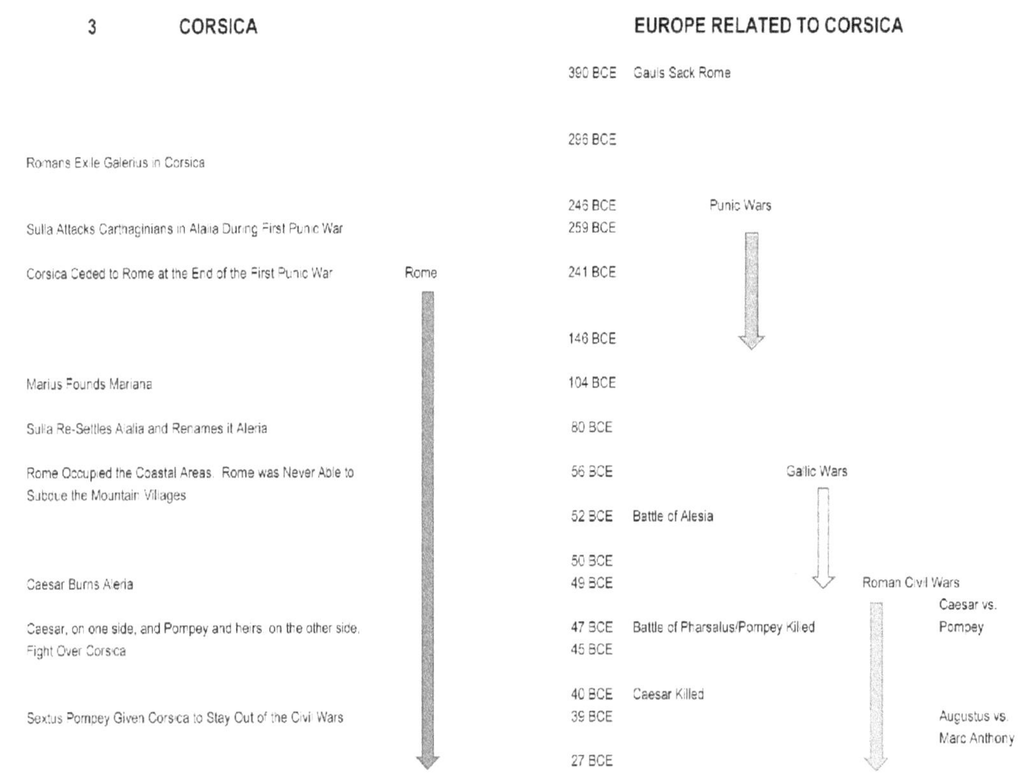
3   CORSICA
EUROPE RELATED TO CORSICA
390 BCE   Gauls Sack Rome
296 BCE
Romans Exile Galerius in Corsica
246 BCE   Punic Wars
Sulla Attacks Carthaginians in Alalia During First Punic War
259 BCE
Corsica Ceded to Rome at the End of the First Punic War   Rome   241 BCE
146 BCE
Marius Founds Mariana   104 BCE
Sulla Re-Settles Alalia and Renames it Aleria   80 BCE
Rome Occupied the Coastal Areas. Rome was Never Able to   56 BCE   Gallic Wars
Subdue the Mountain Villages
52 BCE   Battle of Alesia
50 BCE
Caesar Burns Aleria   49 BCE   Roman Civil Wars
Caesar vs.
Caesar, on one side, and Pompey and heirs on the other side,   47 BCE   Battle of Pharsalus/Pompey Killed   Pompey
Fight Over Corsica   45 BCE
40 BCE   Caesar Killed
Sextus Pompey Given Corsica to Stay Out of the Civil Wars   39 BCE   Augustus vs.
Marc Anthony
27 BCE

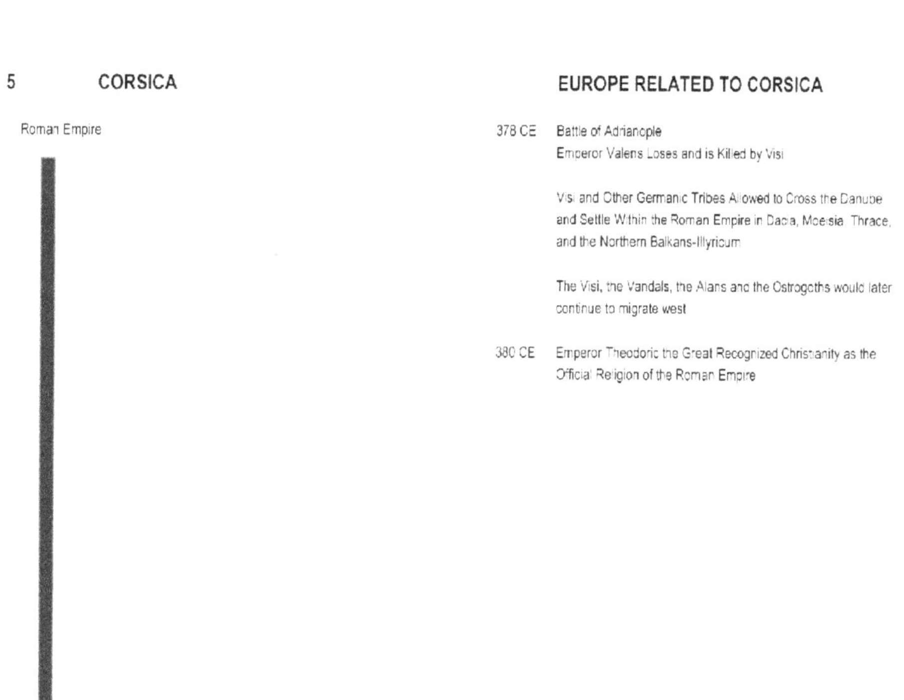

4   CORSICA

Augustus Completes Building Project in Aleria

Roman Empire

Seneca in Exile in Corsica

Otho Holds Corsica

Corsica was a Breadbasket for Rome and Provided Wood for Ships Emperors and the Senate Traded Administration of Corsica

St. Devota Martyred

Corsica was Administered by the Praetorian Guard and Maxentius Who Fought and Lost to Constantine

EUROPE RELATED TO CORSICA

27BCE — Start of the Roman Empire — Augustus is Emperor

40 CE — Expansion of the Roman Empire

46 CE

69 CE

303 CE

312 CE — Battle of Milvian Bridge
Constantine Becomes Emperor
Constantine becomes Emperor of the West and the East

313 CE — Edict of Toleration
Christianity Formally Recognized

325 CE — Council of Nicaea
Rejected the Arian Doctrine of the Humanity of Jesus Christ
Most Germanic Tribes were Arian Christians

355 CE — Restoration of Neo-Platonism and Persecution of Christians

365 CE

---

5   CORSICA

Roman Empire

EUROPE RELATED TO CORSICA

378 CE — Battle of Adrianople
Emperor Valens Loses and is Killed by Visi

Visi and Other Germanic Tribes Allowed to Cross the Danube and Settle Within the Roman Empire in Dacia, Moesia Thrace, and the Northern Balkans-Illyricum

The Visi, the Vandals, the Alans and the Ostrogoths would later continue to migrate west

380 CE — Emperor Theodoric the Great Recognized Christianity as the Official Religion of the Roman Empire

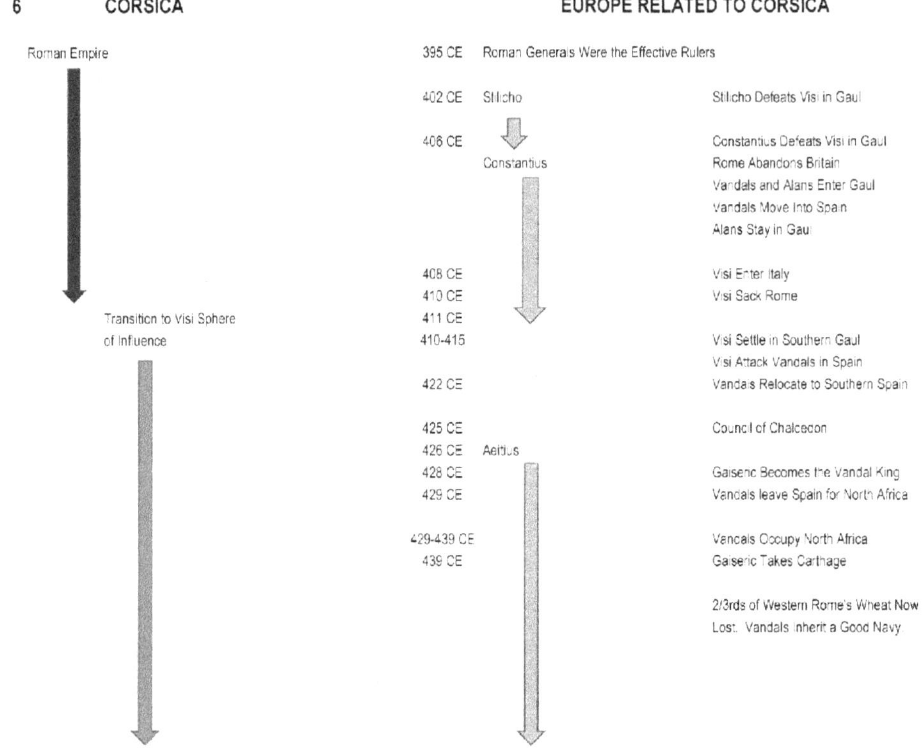

6   CORSICA

EUROPE RELATED TO CORSICA

Roman Empire

395 CE   Roman Generals Were the Effective Rulers

402 CE   Stilicho   Stilicho Defeats Visi in Gaul

406 CE   Constantius   Constantius Defeats Visi in Gaul
Rome Abandons Britain
Vandals and Alans Enter Gaul
Vandals Move Into Spain
Alans Stay in Gaul

408 CE   Visi Enter Italy
410 CE   Visi Sack Rome
411 CE
410-415   Visi Settle in Southern Gaul
Visi Attack Vandals in Spain
422 CE   Vandals Relocate to Southern Spain

425 CE   Council of Chalcedon
426 CE   Aetius
428 CE   Gaiseric Becomes the Vandal King
429 CE   Vandals leave Spain for North Africa

429-439 CE   Vandals Occupy North Africa
439 CE   Gaiseric Takes Carthage

2/3rds of Western Rome's Wheat Now
Lost. Vandals Inherit a Good Navy

Transition to Visi Sphere
of Influence

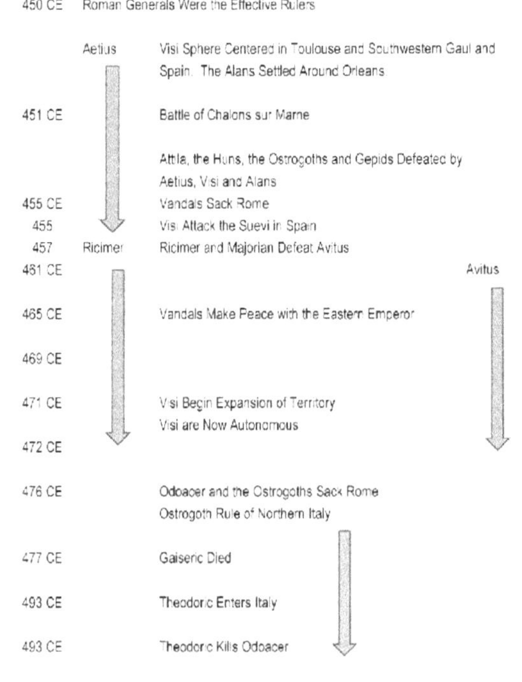

7   CORSICA

EUROPE RELATED TO CORSICA

450 CE   Roman Generals Were the Effective Rulers

Visi Sphere
of Interest

Aetius   Visi Sphere Centered in Toulouse and Southwestern Gaul and
Spain. The Alans Settled Around Orleans

Visi Did Not Try to Integrate into Corsican
Culture. They Maintained their Own
Identity. They Replicated Roman
administration, including the Use of Latin.

451 CE   Battle of Chalons sur Marne

Attila, the Huns, the Ostrogoths and Gepids Defeated by
Aetius, Visi and Alans

Ricimer Defeats the Vandals in Corsica

455 CE   Vandals Sack Rome
455   Visi Attack the Suevi in Spain
457   Ricimer   Ricimer and Majorian Defeat Avitus
461 CE   Avitus

Vandals Attack Aleria

465 CE   Vandals Make Peace with the Eastern Emperor

Vandals Take Corsica

469 CE

Vandals

471 CE   Visi Begin Expansion of Territory
Visi are Now Autonomous

472 CE

Vandals Could Not Conquer the
Interior of Corsica

476 CE   Odoacer and the Ostrogoths Sack Rome
Ostrogoth Rule of Northern Italy

Vandals did Occupy the Coastal Areas and
Referred to Their Occupation as the Kingdom
of the Vandals

477 CE   Gaiseric Died

493 CE   Theodoric Enters Italy

The Vandals Conducted a Similar Type of
Administration as the Visi. Both Administrators Did Not
Rely Upon Taxes Like the Romans and Byzantines.

493 CE   Theodoric Kills Odoacer

8   CORSICA

EUROPE RELATED TO CORSICA

Vandals

495 CE   Battle of Mount Baden in Britain

496 CE   Clovis of the Franks Converts to Orthodox Christianity
Visi, Alans and Vandals are Still Arian Christians

507 CE   Battle of Vouillé   Birth of Modern France
Clovis Defeats the Visi
Visi Lose Toulouse and Retain Just Narbo and Spain

507-526 CE   Consolidation of Frankish Power

Corsica Annexed to the Byzantine Empire

533-535 CE   Belisarius and the Byzantine Army Defeat Vandals

Byzantines

Byzantine Taxes Creates Riots in Corsica

540 CE   Belisarius Defeats Theodoric

Ostrogoths

Totila and Franks Use Corsica for Revolt Against the Byzantines
Narses Quells Revolt

Totila Revolts Against The Byzantines
541   Narses Quells Revolt

Byzantines

Corsica is Administered from the Exarchate of Carthage

568 CE   Lombards Enter Italy

Lombards become Interested in Corsica

580 CE

9   CORSICA

EUROPE RELATED TO CORSICA

The Administration of Corsica is Transferred from the Exarchate of
Carthage to the Exarchate of Ravenna

695 CE   Umayyad Caliphate Defeat the Byzantines in North Africa

711 CE   Umayyad Caliphate Occupies Most of Spain
Mainly Berbers with Some Arab Leaders

712 CE   Luitprand and the Lombards Ally with the Franks Against the
Byzantines

1st Muslim Attack on Corsica
Muslim Raids and Attacks

713 CE

Umayyad Raids

730 CE   Muslims Enter Aquitaine

732 CE   Battle of Tours

Charles Martel and the Franks Along with the Aquitaine Defeat
the Muslims

739 CE   Pippin Defeats Moors at Marseilles
744 CE   End of Lombard-Frankish Alliance

Abbasids Raids

750 CE
751 CE   Lombards Take Exarchate of Ravenna
Pippin Crowned King of the Franks by the Franks

Lombards Enter Corsica

754 CE   Pippin Crowned by Pope Stephen

Papal Interest in Corsica

773 CE

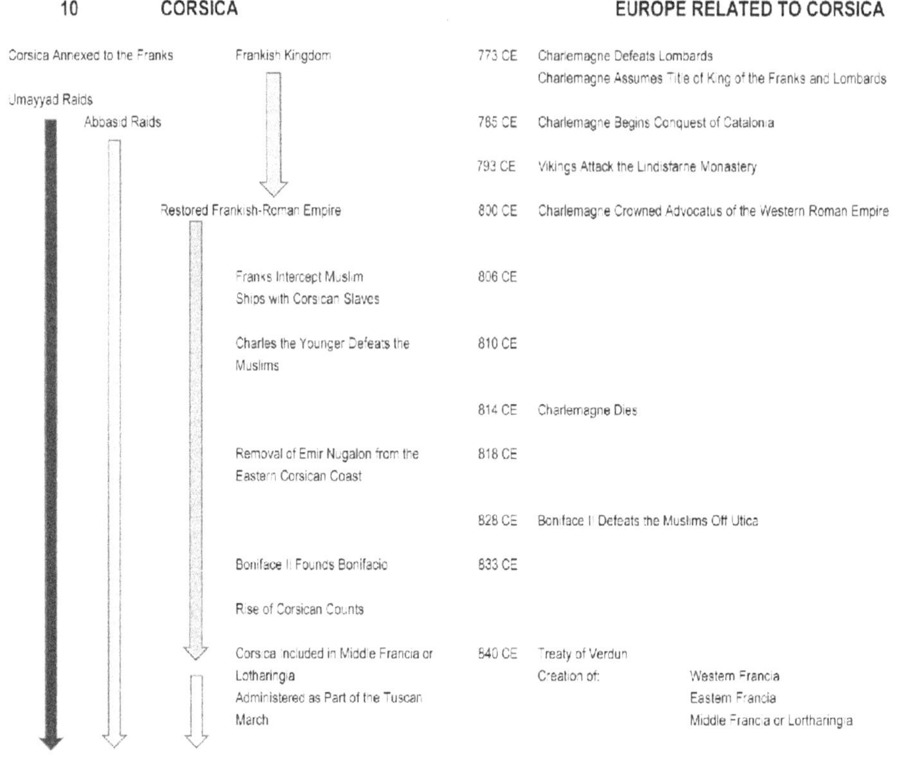
10   CORSICA
EUROPE RELATED TO CORSICA
Corsica Annexed to the Franks
Frankish Kingdom
Umayyad Raids
Abbasid Raids
773 CE   Charlemagne Defeats Lombards
Charlemagne Assumes Title of King of the Franks and Lombards
785 CE   Charlemagne Begins Conquest of Catalonia
793 CE   Vikings Attack the Lindisfarne Monastery
Restored Frankish-Roman Empire
800 CE   Charlemagne Crowned Advocatus of the Western Roman Empire
Franks Intercept Muslim
Ships with Corsican Slaves
806 CE
Charles the Younger Defeats the
Muslims
810 CE
814 CE   Charlemagne Dies
Removal of Emir Nugalon from the
Eastern Corsican Coast
818 CE
828 CE   Boniface II Defeats the Muslims Off Utica
Boniface II Founds Bonifacio
833 CE
Rise of Corsican Counts
Corsica Included in Middle Francia or
Lotharingia
Administered as Part of the Tuscan
March
840 CE   Treaty of Verdun
Creation of: Western Francia
Eastern Francia
Middle Francia or Lortharingia

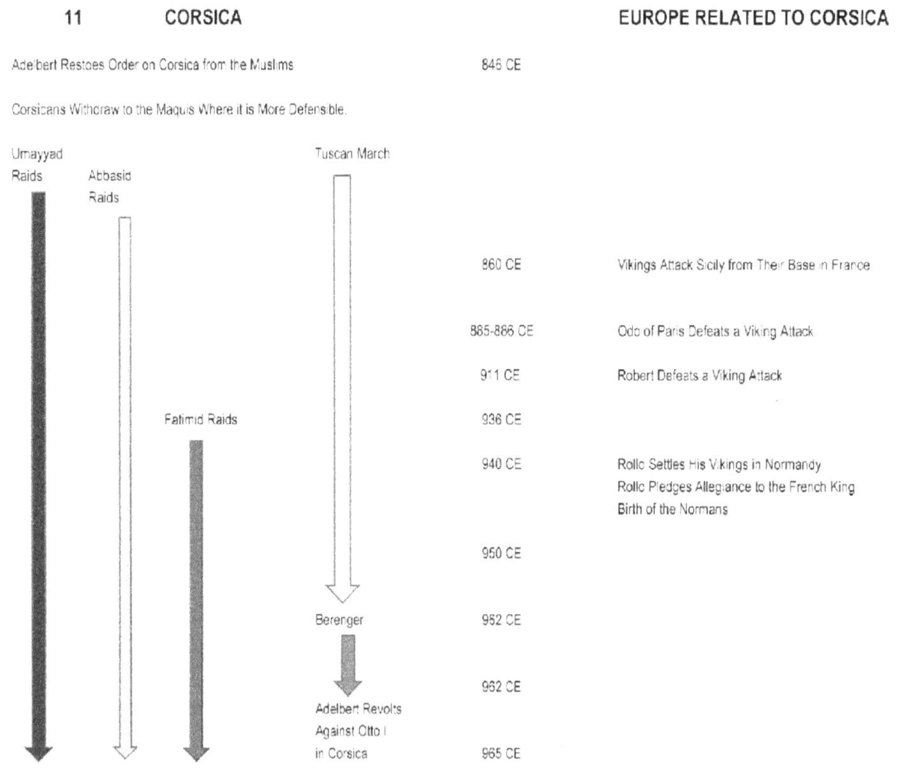
11   CORSICA
EUROPE RELATED TO CORSICA
Adelbert Restores Order on Corsica from the Muslims
846 CE
Corsicans Withdraw to the Maquis Where it is More Defensible.
Umayyad
Raids
Abbasid
Raids
Tuscan March
860 CE   Vikings Attack Sicily from Their Base in France
885-886 CE   Odo of Paris Defeats a Viking Attack
911 CE   Robert Defeats a Viking Attack
936 CE
Fatimid Raids
940 CE   Rollo Settles His Vikings in Normandy
Rollo Pledges Allegiance to the French King
Birth of the Normans
950 CE
Berenger   962 CE
962 CE
Adelbert Revolts
Against Otto I
in Corsica   965 CE

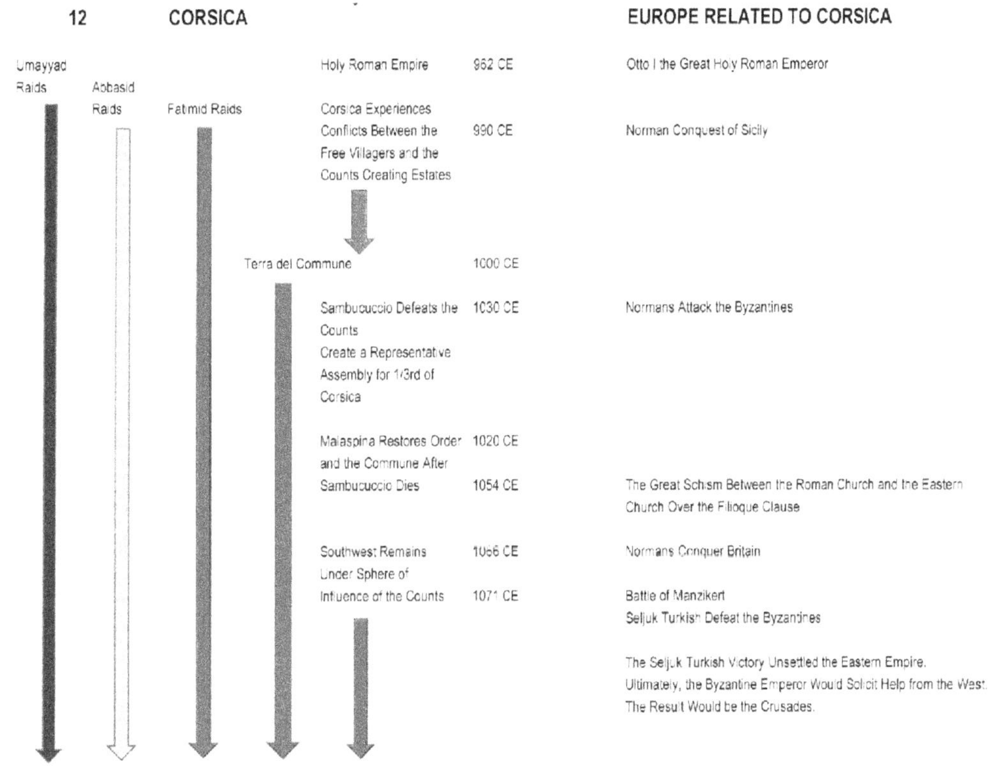
12
CORSICA
EUROPE RELATED TO CORSICA
Umayyad Raids
Abbasid Raids
Fatimid Raids
Holy Roman Empire
962 CE
Otto I the Great Holy Roman Emperor
Corsica Experiences Conflicts Between the Free Villagers and the Counts Creating Estates
990 CE
Norman Conquest of Sicily
Terra del Commune
1000 CE
Sambucuccio Defeats the Counts
Create a Representative Assembly for 1/3rd of Corsica
1030 CE
Normans Attack the Byzantines
Malaspina Restores Order and the Commune After Sambucuccio Dies
1020 CE
1054 CE
The Great Schism Between the Roman Church and the Eastern Church Over the Filioque Clause
Southwest Remains Under Sphere of Influence of the Counts
1066 CE
Normans Conquer Britain
1071 CE
Battle of Manzikert
Seljuk Turkish Defeat the Byzantines
The Seljuk Turkish Victory Unsettled the Eastern Empire. Ultimately, the Byzantine Emperor Would Solicit Help from the West. The Result Would be the Crusades.

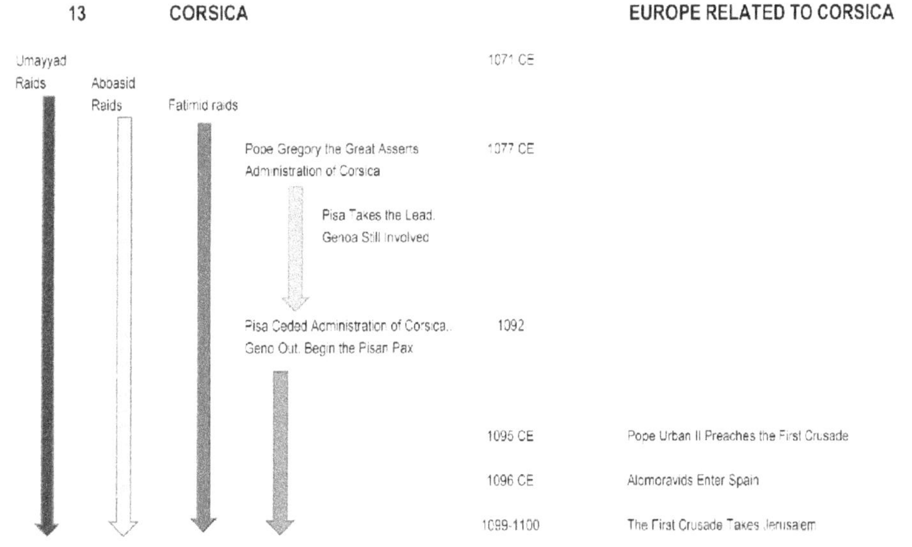
13
CORSICA
EUROPE RELATED TO CORSICA
Umayyad Raids
Abbasid Raids
Fatimid raids
1071 CE
Pope Gregory the Great Asserts Administration of Corsica
1077 CE
Pisa Takes the Lead. Genoa Still Involved
Pisa Ceded Administration of Corsica. Geno Out. Begin the Pisan Pax
1092
1095 CE
Pope Urban II Preaches the First Crusade
1096 CE
Almoravids Enter Spain
1099-1100
The First Crusade Takes Jerusalem

9 781958 004807